THE KING AND HIS VIGILANT VALET

PARANORMAL PRINCES BOOK 3

CHARLIE COCHET

SYNOPSIS

JEAN

The past has a way of catching up with you, even if you are immortal. I've spent thousands of years as the valet and companion to the powerful King of All Shifters. It has been my honor and duty to protect, serve, and advise him. I never intended to fall in love with him. My past is filled with death and bloodshed, but I never once regretted keeping Alarick safe. Now an evil I thought long gone has resurfaced, determined to kill Alarick and plunge the world into chaos. Saving Alarick means revealing the truth about myself. I don't know what's worse, failing to protect the king I love, or watching him turn away from me in disgust when he discovers what I really am.

KING ALARICK

As King of All Shifters, my powers are connected to the cosmos, and I have been around since the dawn of time. There are few things that can kill me. Unfortunately, one of those things has escaped its prison and is set to destroy me. The only weapon that can defeat this creature is the Scythe of Kronos, which has been missing for nearly as long as I have lived. When Jean and I set out on a quest to find the scythe, questions I had long ignored must now be answered. What is Jean's connection to this evil? Why will he trust me with his life but not his secrets? As my most trusted valet and my greatest friend, surely nothing that happens along this perilous journey can change what I feel in my heart for him. Or can it?

PROLOGUE

JEAN

"You should get into bed, Your Majesty."

Alarick groaned as he valiantly fought sleep, his eyelids lowering. "Not yet."

I held back a smile and continued to run my fingers through his hair. This had become a nightly ritual of ours, one initiated by him, I might add. After a long day, I would sit on the couch in his royal chambers, and he would lie down, stretching his long body and resting his head on my lap.

"Just a few more minutes," he mumbled, his words laced with sleep.

Alarick fell asleep on my lap so often, I could count the heartbeats it took for him to go under. His head was tilted slightly back, dark stubble growing on his handsome face. He wasn't traditionally beautiful. His features were rugged —a square jaw, little creases at the corners of his eyes from thousands of years of smiling. His hair had grown to around his ears again, and soon it would be time for a trim. It warmed me, knowing I was the only one he allowed to cut his hair. His full lips were slightly parted, his features softened in sleep. With a feathery touch, I brushed my fingers down his cheek to his jaw, smiling at the sigh he released. He turned onto his side toward me and snuggled close.

When had this complicated, inexplicable, perplexing creature become my very reason for breathing? How had he become my *everything*? It made no sense. He was a king. *The* King of All Shifters. His power was vast, connected to the stars above, evident by the swirling cosmos reflected in his fathomless eyes. He could shift into any animal he'd fathered since the beginning of time, yet most days he needed me to find his socks. Some days I wondered how he'd survived all those years before I became his advisor and valet. He had the most outlandish thoughts, had *no* impulse control, ate far too many sweets, and was spoiled rotten. Yet he possessed a pure-hearted kindness I had come across in so few. A genuine love for his children and the world they inhabited.

"Still here?"

Alarick's hand over my heart stilled me, as it did every time. He had a habit of placing his hand over that spot and did it more often than he realized. I was almost as familiar with Alarick's touch as I was my own, and I lived for those moments. They flayed me open, exposing the raw nerve that was my love for him, but I wouldn't give them up for anything. I yearned for those tender touches, basked in them, and was fortunate they came often. My presence soothed him, and after thousands of years together, having me near was a comfort to him. I'd become more than his valet. I'd become his companion. Yet he sought reassurance of my presence. More often than not, some part of him rested against me, and if he couldn't, he'd find his way around to it by placing a hand on my knee, my shoulder, my chest. He had absolutely no idea what he did to me with those touches.

I covered his hand with mine and murmured a softly spoken, "Always."

"Good." Alarick hummed, drifting off, most likely telling himself he'd only take a nap.

With a warm smile, I continued to run my fingers through his soft hair. I held on to his hand and enjoyed this moment, letting its warmth flood through me. My eyes closed, and I balanced on the edge of sleep. Suddenly a presence I'd not felt in a very long time jolted me alert. My heart lurched, and I stilled. It wasn't possible.

Carefully I slipped out from underneath Alarick, then headed for the balcony. The guards posted outside the door and in the hall would keep watch over him. No need to alarm them until I investigated. Closing the balcony doors behind me, I sniffed the air, my blood turning to ice. After thousands of years, it couldn't be.

I pulled loose the bandage from around my eyes and peered out in the direction of the forest beyond the garden. It was an old habit, but it helped ground me. For thousands of years, I'd honed my senses and magic to replace the sight I'd lost. I searched the darkness, startled by the putrid magic pulsing from within the thickness of the trees, which along with the pitch-black shadows helped shroud the presence.

Please, let me be wrong about this.

Jumping over the balcony, I landed without a sound on the grass below. I stalked in silence toward the trees, listening for any hint of what might be out there. A green glow pulsed in the darkness before me, and a gasp escaped my lips before I could stop it.

"Who are you?" I demanded, knowing I didn't have to raise my voice to be heard. Not by the creature lurking in the woods.

"You don't recognize one of your own?" The voice was gravelly, drawn-out. "You wound me."

"Lies," I hissed. "I am the last of my kind."

"So you believed."

"So I *know*." I stepped forward, fingers flexing at the ready. No one dared step foot on the palace grounds with the intent to harm Alarick, not since I became his valet and promised a swift death to anyone foolish enough to make an attempt.

"Perhaps you were. For a time. I'd been trapped by magic and frozen for thousands of years, but not dead. I am finally free."

I moved closer, the familiarity of the voice tickling a long-forgotten memory. Many lifetimes had passed since they'd all left this mortal world, yet I knew this voice. "How is this possible?"

"Global warming. It's a thing, apparently. Hooray for me."

"Is that a joke? Never mind. I don't care."

"You should. It was *your* war that saw me end up there, frozen and imprisoned inside that cursed mountain, thawing year by year, weak and starving, feeding off whatever magical creatures came along. Like scraps thrown to a dog."

I froze. Espen Mountain. "You killed the bear shifter prince and then tried to kill his son."

"By the time the first prince appeared, enough of me had thawed that I could feed properly. I then bided my time. When the son returned, I'd all but thawed. He would have made a tasty snack before my journey here, but sadly he escaped. No matter."

"Why are you here?" The question was redundant. I knew why he was here. I only needed him to confirm it so I could rid the world of him once and for all, as I had so many of the others.

"You know why I'm here."

The blood in my veins turned to ice. "Your king is dead. Has been dead for nearly as long as you've been frozen."

"Yes, but the mission lives, and I will see it finished."

"I forbid it!" My power coursed through me, green sparks of lightning jumping from one finger to another. I flinched at the sting. It had been so long since I'd needed to summon the death within me. The evil, rolling laugh that echoed around me had me gritting my teeth and hissing.

"You have no power over me. Tell me, does your precious king know who you are? *What* you are? Does he know why you came to him?"

I ignored the taunt. Alarick would never know, if I had anything to say on the matter. "I won't let you touch him."

"Look at you! Pathetic. Your true power is gone."

The voice echoed from somewhere on my right, and I turned in that direction. "I don't need my sight to defeat you."

"Oh, but you do, and we both know it."

I shook my head despite the fear swirling inside me.

"Yes." The evil laugh grew louder, closer, now somewhere to the left. "Your sight was the source of your greatest power."

My heart stuttered, and I faltered before quickly regaining my fortitude. I would not allow him to poison my mind. "Show yourself, and I will gladly acquaint you with what little power I have left!"

A green glow pulsed, and I readied myself, but it suddenly vanished. Frowning, I edged closer to the woods. Nothing but silence met my ears, a scentless soft breeze ruffling my hair. My muscles tensed at what I heard. No songs from the night birds, chirps from crickets, or fluttering of fairy wings. The world stilled, every sound fading into empty nothingness. He was preparing for the attack.

A blast of green fire knocked me off my feet, the intense heat and pain forcing a cry out of me. My arm throbbed, and I pushed myself to my knees, the scent of my blood in the air. My head swam, my thoughts hazy from the venom coursing through me. The bastard was as strong as I remembered, and no doubt growing stronger, while I had lost a good deal of my power.

"Jean?"

Before I could register what I'd heard, a second green glow pulsed through the trees, and the earth trembled beneath me. I felt him then, as I always did when he was near or in distress. No...

Alarick.

The cosmos shifted around us as Alarick pulled the light toward him, then sent a blast into the darkness, the grass and trees nearly torn from their roots by the explosion.

"Jean!"

"Alarick, no!" I pushed to my feet before turning to face the evil in the forest, my words intended for Alarick. "Go back inside!" Damn the bloody stubborn bastard! He ignored my order, reaching my side and gasping, no doubt at my bloodied state. "Damn it, Alarick, I said go back inside!"

"You must be mad if you think I'm going to leave you out here on your own to face whatever's done this to you."

The forest glowed again, and I turned, throwing myself at him and knocking us both to the grass as the powerful rush of green flames exploded over where we'd stood.

"Run! Into the palace. Now!"

Alarick squeezed my good arm. "Not without you," he said through his teeth.

"Stubborn bastard," I ground out, making him grin.

"It's like you don't know me."

"Come on, then." I grabbed him and pulled him up with me, mumbling under my breath about how he was a pain in my ass.

We ran into the palace, and I shouted at the guards to fortify the gate. I didn't put anything past the vile creature outside and doubted he would wait long before attempting to infiltrate the palace. I pulled Alarick with me, his hand in mine, and I didn't release him until I had him safely locked in the throne room, windows and doors barred, warded by magic. Safe for the moment, I slumped down into a chair as my body healed itself. Alarick knelt before me, his concern for me emanating from him like the warm glow of a fire.

"Jean, talk to me. What's going on? What was that out there?"

I put my hand to his cheek. "I swear to you, I won't let anyone touch you. Not while there's breath in my body."

"Jean?" Alarick leaned into my touch, and a piece of my heart splintered, knowing he would recoil from me if he ever discovered the truth. "You're scaring me now. What's happening?"

"He's here to do the job I never could." I closed my eyes, the past looming over me like a dark storm, threatening to tear apart everything I had built with Alarick. I had a life with him, and even if he couldn't love me the way I did him, simply being at his side brought me more joy than I had ever dreamed possible.

"Job? What job?"

"Of killing you."

Alarick stilled, the image of his beautiful face at times so clear I almost saw him, as if I were looking through glass. If I focused my magic, I might see every detail, but it meant opening myself up, leaving myself completely vulnerable, something I could not afford at this moment. I had to focus all my power on keeping him safe.

"I don't understand."

I opened my mouth to reply, but thunder cracked the skies apart. No, not thunder. It was *him*. He was trying to get in.

"We need to leave." I jumped to my feet and took hold of his arm.

"Nonsense. Whatever it is, I can deal with it. I want to know what you were referring to."

Damn it all. Why did he have to be so stubborn? "Please, Your Majesty. Your life is in danger."

He waved a hand in dismissal. "I cannot be killed."

"We both know that's not true." He might be immortal, but even the gods could be killed. There was always a way, and one of them was trying to crash through the gates.

Alarick turned to me and cupped my face. "Jean, are you saying whatever is out there was sent to kill me and has the power to do so?"

"Yes! That's exactly what I'm saying. It's what I've been saying for the past several minutes!"

"Has anyone told you how adorable you look when you're indignant?"

I opened my mouth to reply, but no response was forthcoming. Adorable? I loathed the very idea of it, yet I melted a little because he was the one who thought so. Goddess above, I was going mad. *He* was driving me to madness. I finally found my voice and smacked his hands away. "Why are you laughing? What is there to laugh about? Someone has been sent to *kill* you, and you're blathering nonsense!"

Alarick chuckled, and my brows shot up. Really? He nodded, and for several heartbeats I focused my magic to see his smile turning into a forced frown as he *pretended* not to be amused. "Yes, right. Serious."

I was going to strangle him with his robe sash. With a growl, I grabbed his arm and pointed ahead. "The cabin in Svalbard. Take us there now."

"Svalbard? Oh no. It's cold there. And we both know how Princess Sinopa feels about me."

On a good day, the Princess of the Arctic Fox Shifters wanted to bury Alarick in the snow. I was starting to understand her sentiments on the matter.

"Your Majesty," I ground out through my teeth as another *boom* rocked the palace around us, "do you trust me?"

"With my life," he replied, sounding offended by the question.

"Then do as I say."

"I can't leave our staff."

"They will be safe. It's you he wants. Now open a portal."

"Jean—"

Another thunderous boom erupted. "Alarick, open the damn portal *now*!"

"All right. But I expect an explanation when we get there." With a flick of his wrist, he opened a portal, and I ceased all use of my magic before I not so gently shoved him through. It closed behind us in a swirl of ice and snow. I couldn't see him glare at me, but I certainly felt it. Adverse weather conditions played havoc with my senses anyway, making it more difficult for my magic to help me "see," so there was no point in taking the risk. Despite our current predicament, I held back a smile when Alarick wrapped his arm around my shoulders to lead me in the right direction.

Tragically underdressed for the bitter cold, we shivered as the ice and wind whipped at our skin. A few more steps and we'd be at the cozy log cabin in the middle of snowy nowhere, but I felt the cold down to my bones. Alarick could have shifted into a polar bear or any number of creatures acclimated to the cold, but he didn't in order to guide me. I had the power to summon heat, but any use of my magic would alert *him*, exposing our location, and I couldn't have that.

Finally inside the cabin, I brushed the snow off myself and hurried to the fireplace to get a fire started. My entire body trembled as I rubbed my hands together, waiting for the flames to grow. Alarick pressed himself to my back, and I stilled.

"What are you doing?"

"Warming us up while you get that going." He rubbed at my arms, the warmth of his chest against my back sending heat greater than any blaze flaring through me.

The only sound around us came from the howling wind outside and the crackling kindle in the fireplace. Alarick let his chin rest on my shoulder, his mouth so close to my face his breath warmed my skin.

"Are you warm now?"

Unable to bring myself to speak, I merely nodded. He stepped away, and I wished I'd not replied at all. I sensed him somewhere to my left and heard the shift of fabric as he sat on the love seat. He patted the space next to him.

"Come sit. There's a nice warm blanket here."

Closing my eyes, I attempted to push down the fear that threatened to rise up and take control. I turned, took a step forward, and stubbed my toe.

"Damnation!"

"Goodness, Jean. What's the matter?"

"I'm bloody blind," I snapped at him. "In case you haven't noticed."

"You once led an entire army through a poisonous maze filled with terrifying creatures, without a single casualty. Are you telling me you can't maneuver around an ottoman?"

Breathe.

Teeth gritted, I joined him on the love seat, mindful not to run into any more damned furniture. I sat at the end of it out of habit, and he didn't hesitate. He lay back, his head on my lap and his knees bent because he was too tall to stretch out. I closed my eyes and allowed myself to absorb his warmth. The tension fled from my body at an embarrassing rate. His effect on me was instant.

"Well?"

And the tension was back. "We should be safe here," I murmured, placing a hand on his brow.

"You're stalling."

He knew me too well. I supposed there was no avoiding it, considering we'd fled the palace.

"Why don't we start with whoever *he* is." Alarick didn't move from where he lay, but I felt his gaze on me.

"His name is Nathair. I thought he was dead, but apparently he'd been trapped in Espen Mountain."

Alarick went rigid. "Wait. Did he—"

"Kill Bernd's father and then try to kill Bernd? Yes, that was Nathair. He'd been slowly thawing, feeding off magical creatures who drew close enough until he could be free. We have humans to thank for that." Who knew what else was out there, lying in wait for the damage to be done so it could once again be free to unleash chaos?

"Who is he?"

"An assassin," I replied, moving my hand from his brow.

"Like you."

I flinched. It wasn't a question, but a statement. I nodded.

"You were sent to kill me."

"Yes."

"And instead you saved my life."

My smile held no humor. "Not a very good assassin."

"Jean, there is nothing you don't excel at. Try again."

His words warmed me and chilled me all at once. "You're right. I was the very best at what I did." Those years were a blur to me now, a distant fog in the depths of my mind. I had been something else back then. Something... monstrous. "You became my mission. I was sent to infiltrate your kingdom, learn about your powers, how many shifter children you had, and how they came into being. I was to get to know you and become your friend."

"Which you did exceptionally well."

His tone held no harshness or malice, which made me feel all the worse. I didn't deserve his kindness.

"At first I was eager to get it done. To return home and declare my victory." I tentatively brushed my fingers over his lips. "I never expected to be the one struck down. You confounded me, and with every smile, you unraveled my binding until all I could see... was you."

CHAPTER ONE

ALARICK

I SAT UP, deeply touched by Jean's soft-spoken words. He looked so vulnerable then, an image at odds with the skilled warrior who had defeated hordes in my defense. It all became clear now, his sudden appearance in my life so many years ago. I'd been drawn to him, intrigued by the mysterious creature with sparkling aquamarine eyes, their depths fathomless, drawing me in, almost... hypnotizing.

"I remember," I said, thinking back to that bright and beautiful day in Crete. "I held court on the steps of the palace at Knossos. You wore a red-and-blue loincloth, with bronze bands on your wrists."

"And you were dressed to rival the king with your colorful loincloth and detailed cloak, sitting there looking regal, larger than life. As if you were a god sent to be worshiped by mortals. And they did worship you, following you everywhere you went, offering gifts."

"You flatter me, Jean. I simply told a good story." Though admittedly, I never corrected their beliefs that I was a god, or godlike. I'd been born from the very heavens themselves when the world was new. "I remember thinking, what a handsome fellow. Nice legs." I smiled at Jean's startled laugh. His cheeks turned a lovely shade of pink. He really had no idea how handsome he was. Quickly brushing that thought aside, I positioned myself closer to him, one arm resting on the back of the love seat behind his head. "At first I thought you were seeking me out for a little merriment."

Jean didn't reply, but his lips quirked up in one corner. Cheeky devil.

"When you came over, I was expecting some sort of invitation, but instead you sat and merely listened. For hours, you sat with me. When the sun set and no one was left but the two of us, you asked to escort me home." It had been incredibly sweet, especially since I knew him to be some kind of magical creature, which meant he could smell what I was. He'd been so shy, rarely making eye contact, and when he did, a heartbeat later his eyes were darting away. "We had the loveliest walk through the gardens."

Jean hummed.

"You were so dark and mysterious, and yet I enjoyed your company immensely. After that, you spent every moment at my side."

"I kept telling myself soon, soon I would kill you."

I smiled. "Centuries went by, and you remained at my side as I moved from one place to another. Then came the day that changed my life."

"Panathenaea," Jean murmured. "The Parthenon."

"A beautiful summer's day in Athens. The breeze ruffling the leaves of the olive trees, the sun's rays warm against my skin. You wore a blue-and-gold chiton, with leather bands on your wrists."

"And you wore a red-and-gold cloak."

"We had fun that day, didn't we? Eating, drinking, dancing." I nudged Jean's arm, and he chuckled. "Remember the dancing?"

"How could I forget? I was awful."

"You were..." I tried to find the right word.

"Awkward?"

"Courageous."

He laughed. "Is that what we're calling it?"

I'd surprised Jean by asking him to dance, and promptly discovered Jean had never danced before. I'd asked him plenty of times previously, but he always came up with one excuse or another, and I finally understood why. He'd been so embarrassed. It was sweet.

"You spent the rest of the evening teaching me when you should have been enjoying yourself," Jean grumbled.

"And who says I didn't enjoy myself?"

Jean tilted his head toward me, a little smile playing on his lips. He really had no clue how charming he was. Where on earth were these thoughts coming from? I'd never thought of Jean in such a fashion. He was my dearest friend. I pulled my arm from around his neck and patted his thigh.

"We walked home that evening. It was quite late, and I was a little... merry."

Jean's snort was most indelicate. "You were three sheets to the wind."

"Was I? I don't recall."

"Of course you don't," he said, his voice filled with amusement.

"Right. So, I was merry, and you so kindly escorted me home. You also helped me into bed, removing my sandals.

Far easier than the ruffled collars we had to deal with years later in London. Remember those?"

"I hated those blasted things," Jean griped. "I swear, with every passing monarch, human fashion grew more stifling and ridiculous."

"You had a smashing beard, though." I rubbed at his clean-shaven jaw, and I could have sworn I heard him purr. "Anyway, back to Athens. You helped me into bed, where I quickly passed out."

"From your merriment," he reminded me with a teasing smile.

"Yes. When I woke, it was to the sight of four dead ruffians sprawled on the floor in pools of their own blood. What an awful smell." Whatever manner of creature they'd been remained a mystery. "You saved my life, Jean, and in gratitude I offered you whatever you wanted." I hadn't known what to expect, but I certainly hadn't expected the words that came from his mouth.

"I want nothing but to serve you," Jean said softly.

His words squeezed at my heart, and I patted his leg again. "That's what you said. Let's return to the whole 'you were sent to kill me' part. Who sent you?"

"Your Majesty—"

My anger boiled. "That's enough of that," I snapped.

"I beg your pardon?"

I never lost my temper with him. Never. "I might act the fool at times, Jean, but I'm no fool. You call me that to keep me at a distance. We've been together for far too long, mean far too much to each other for you to insist on such formalities. I've had enough. You will call me Alarick."

Jean nodded. "Very well."

"Who sent you?"

"My king. Or rather, my former king."

"Who is...?" I prompted and waited. Jean was like a vault when it came to secrets. An admirable trait, but an infuriating one as well, especially when *I* was the one in need of information.

"Dead. Has been dead for a very long time."

"Right. And he was...?"

"Not important."

My sigh was very heavy. "I see what you're doing."

"Do you?"

"Yes. Very well. So you were an assassin, and your king sent you to kill me."

"Correct."

"Why?"

"You were teaching your children to cohabit with humans. He was not a fan. Your shifter children outnumbered all magical creatures, and he feared you would create an army that could defeat him, keep him from throwing the world into chaos, allowing him and our kind to reign over all."

"Very ambitious, this former king of yours. All right. You went against his orders to kill me, and instead saved me. How did he take it?"

"Not well. He sent several of his assassins to kill me and finish the mission."

I frowned at this. "I never saw them."

"Because I killed them before they could get anywhere near you. I let it be known that anyone who tried to harm you would meet a swift and merciless death."

I had no doubt he'd made good on his threats. "How many assassins did you kill for me, Jean?"

"All but one."

"Nathair. Because he was frozen."

"That's correct."

"And your king?"

Jean went quiet for a moment before turning his head in my direction. "Like I said, all but one."

"So much death, Jean." I'd never asked him to kill for me, never expected it, and not once had it occurred to me that Jean was the reason I'd lived for so long without any real threat to my immortal life. How much blood did he have on his hands because of me?

"They were cold-hearted killers. It's what they were born for. What *I* was—*had been* born for."

I suspected there was more to that. Jean might have been born for killing, and I'd never met a fiercer warrior, but all I saw was the loyal friend who brought me soup when I felt melancholy or sat by my side reading a book as I attended to my duties. He took care of me like no other, always gentle and caring.

"All that blood on your hands. For me. Why?"

Jean turned and cupped my face, his thumb brushing my cheek. "Oh, Alarick. Do you really not know?" His smile was soft, his words quiet. "I—"

A pounding on the front door startled us both, and I cursed under my breath for being caught unawares, not to mention for being interrupted. What had Jean been about to say? I stood, and Jean quickly stepped in front of me. I ignored his annoyed huff when I followed him to the door. It's not like we didn't know who stood on the other side.

Jean opened the door, and a dainty girl dressed in white from the white pom-pom on her hat to her white boots, glared at me.

"It's true, then. What are you doing here? Don't you and Lord Eldrich have somewhere else to go get frisky?"

I gaped at her. "What? That's not—"

"I don't care. What are you doing in my kingdom?"

"Um, enjoying your frigidness. I mean your kingdom's frigidness! No, I mean the scenery. Very beautiful. All the snow. Lots of white."

Jean groaned and shoved me to one side. He smiled that brilliant smile of his and took Sinopa's hand in his, bringing it to his lips for a kiss. "Your Highness. Always a pleasure to see you."

Sinopa's sweet smile was genuine. "It's always a pleasure to see you as well, Lord Eldrich." She lifted her gaze to me, and her smile turned into a glower. She ground out what I assumed was meant to be a greeting. "Your Majesty."

Before I could offer a greeting in response, she swept past me into the cabin. Jean closed the door, and I would have sworn he was trying not to smile. She pulled the hat off her head, white hair cascading past her shoulders. She shoved the hat into her pocket along with her gloves, then warmed her hands by the fire. Jean took hold of my arm and pulled me to one side to speak quietly to me.

"You must apologize to her."

"Apologize? That's absurd. I'm the king. I don't apologize." The events of the day must be getting to him. He motioned for me to give him something, and I pulled the sash from around my robe. "Jean, it's not necessary."

He grunted but continued to wrap the purple sash around his eyes. I wished he could see himself the way I saw him. Everything about him was beautiful, but all he saw were his flaws.

"Nonsense," he said, tucking the end of the sash into itself behind his head. "You were wrong. Therefore, you must apologize."

"I was not wrong, Jean. I am never wrong." The very idea had me chuckling. Wrong. Hardly.

"You are. Often."

I frowned at him. That didn't sound right. "Are you sure?"

"Very."

"If you say so. Very well. I will... apologize."

"And learn from your mistakes," he added sweetly.

I narrowed my eyes at him. "And learn from my mistakes." I turned to the princess. "Princess Sinopa, I would like to acknowledge that perhaps I might not have been correct in my assumption that you possessed certain sensibilities and provided you with a perfectly suitable mate, who you rejected quite harshly."

Sinopa's mouth dropped open, but no words were forthcoming. Was that not right? As far as apologies went, I thought it was rather good.

Jean turned to me, mouth hanging open. He leaned in and whispered hoarsely at me, "What was that?"

"An apology."

"No, it wasn't. It was so very not an apology. It was the farthest thing from an apology I've ever heard. Try again."

Very well. "Princess Sinopa. It's my understanding you were offended—"

Jean grabbed my arm and turned me away. "Still no," he hissed. "Goddess above, you are *terrible* at this. Repeat after me. I..."

Easy enough. "I."

"Am."

"Am."

"Sorry."

Hm. I'd heard that word before, but it felt foreign to me. "S... sorry."

"For being a pompous, insensitive jerk, who rather than ask you what *you* wanted, made a terrible assumption based on ignorance. It will never happen again."

"Really, Jean?"

"Say it."

I spun around and put a hand to my heart. "Princess Sinopa. I am so very sorry. I was a pompous, insensitive jerk, who rather than ask you what *you* wanted, made a terrible assumption based on ignorance. It will never happen again."

Sinopa peered at me. "Do you mean it?"

Her hopeful expression squeezed at my heart. I nodded. "I only want to see my children happy. It was terribly wrong of me to assume that signified having a mate. If you—or any of my children—do not wish to be mated, I will respect that decision." I meant every word. All I wanted was their happiness. The world seemed to be moving at breakneck speed these days, and at times I felt as if I were in the center of a whirlwind, the only thing not moving.

Tears welled in her eyes, and she launched herself at me. I jumped with a start, at first believing I'd made the situation worse and she was about to murder me. Seeing as how Jean simply stood there, I relaxed and wrapped my arms around her, confident no maiming was about to occur.

"Thank you," she said with a sniff before pulling away. "I know you like to play matchmaker, but maybe consider that some of us might not want to be matched."

"I'll do better," I promised, and I had every intention of keeping my word. Perhaps it was time I listened to my children. "Goodness. I *had* made a mistake. And I learned from it! Did you see that, Jean?" I beamed proudly, and he smiled, eyes alight with amusement.

Sinopa rolled her eyes, but a smile tugged at her lips. "Okay, so why are you here if it's not to debauch Lord Eldrich?"

I gasped far louder than I should have for a man of my

years. "No one is doing any debauching, and certainly not of Jean!" I felt my face heat and quickly cleared my throat. "Not that he isn't worthy of debauching. I mean, he's very handsome, and strong, and... such. What I mean to say is, that's not our purpose here. Not that it's our purpose elsewhere, or that I plan to debauch Jean at a later point, but—"

"Your Majesty?"

"Yes?"

"Don't hurt yourself. Why are you here?"

Get to the point. Good idea. "Someone is trying to kill me."

She waved a hand in dismissal. "Someone is always trying to kill you. Oh, wait. They're just thinking about it."

"You—"

Jean cleared his throat. Right. Opening mouth without thinking led to more apologies.

"Wait, someone is trying to kill you?" she asked, eyes huge. "Someone who can *actually* kill you is trying to kill you?"

"Yes."

Her face blanched, and I was touched to find she did care, even if at times I was certain she was plotting my demise, or at least considering gnawing at my ankles. Arctic foxes had very sharp little teeth.

"Who are they?" She took a seat on the couch.

"An assassin. One I thought long dead," Jean replied.

Sinopa studied Jean. "Can't you kill him?"

"That would be like someone trying to kill Jean," I offered, drawing her attention back to me.

Her eyes went huge, and realization dawned on her. "This assassin is one of Lord Eldrich's kind."

Sinopa didn't ask what Jean was. No one did. All my shifter children were aware that even I didn't know, and I had a feeling that despite our current situation, Jean wouldn't reveal his true nature either. Why? He trusted me with everything else. Why not this? Did he believe I'd shun him? I had shifter children who were truly terrifying, and I loved them unconditionally. Did he not trust in my affection for him? In our friendship? After all these years?

Jean nodded. "I'm afraid I don't have the power I once did. I can fight him, but in the end, he would kill me."

Sinopa cursed under her breath and ran a hand through her hair. She lifted her gaze to mine, worry in her pale blue eyes. "How are you going to stop him, then?"

"There's only one thing that can stop him," Jean said, his voice quiet. "A weapon of divine slaying, capable of killing a god."

I stared at him. It couldn't be.

"What?" Sinopa asked, looking from me to Jean and back. "What's with the faces?"

"There must be another way," I informed Jean.

"What weapon?" Sinopa asked, frustrated.

Jean didn't respond. Goddess above, it was worse than I thought. I turned to Sinopa. "The weapon we need is known as the Scythe of Kronos, and it's been lost for millenniums. No one knows its whereabouts, not even the gods." Not that it would help us even if they'd known, considering they'd vanished from the Earth a lifetime ago. We were on our own.

CHAPTER TWO

JEAN

"KRONOS? As in King of the Titans. The father of Zeus?" Sinopa asked. "You can't be serious. Wow, I hope I look as good as you two when I'm ancient."

"I'm not ancient," I muttered, resuming my seat on the couch as Sinopa and Alarick argued over his being "ancient," which Alarick was.

I wasn't prone to foolishness, but I never expected my past to catch up with me. Anyone who'd known me, who knew who and what I was, had been dead for almost as long as I'd been at Alarick's side. I should have been more thorough. I'd known Nathair had been dispatched, but I should have hunted down his carcass to be certain. Now Alarick was in great danger.

"Jean?"

Alarick had been speaking to me, and I hadn't heard a word.

"Yes? Forgive me. My mind wandered."

"Are you all right?" he asked, his tone one of concern as he took a seat beside me, our legs touching.

"Yes." I smiled warmly when his hand came to rest on mine. He was never so forward or intimate with anyone else, and it brought joy to my heart. I could pinpoint the exact moment I fell in love with him. That day at the Parthenon when I finally accepted Alarick's invitation to dance was the day everything changed. Little did Alarick know that in that moment when he took my hand in his, bringing our bodies close together, he had injected love and light into what had remained of my cold dark heart. By then, I had been doubting my mission for some time. The King of All Shifters was to be destroyed. He was a plague to our world, as were his children. But the longer I spent around Alarick, the more difficult it became to see him as a monster to be vanquished. I'd never known someone with so much power filled with such unlimited... goodness.

Alarick confounded me from the moment I met him. Here was a godlike creature with what appeared to be infinite power, which he refused to use against anyone, not even those who wished him harm. He had no desire to rule over anyone, not even his shifter children. Unless absolutely necessary, Alarick did not interfere in the lives of his children. He used his powers to help others.

I'd studied Alarick closely after we first met, intent on discovering what made him so dangerous. In my lifetime I had confronted true horrors, and Alarick looked nothing like the monsters I'd killed. But appearances could be deceiving, so I'd stayed close to him, observing him, waiting for the façade to slip. I'd been certain his true nature would reveal itself. I simply had to be patient. Weeks turned into months, and months turned into years, and Alarick remained the same. He brought food to those who had none, helped the injured, offered shelter to those in need. To my kind, Alarick had been regarded as a fool who didn't deserve his power. In my eyes, he became a precious gift to the world.

On our way home from the Parthenon, I realized the perfect opportunity to kill Alarick had presented itself. He had left himself vulnerable, trusting in me completely. After many years together, not only had I earned his trust, but more importantly, I had earned his affection. Alarick might not remember that night, but I would never forget it. He had stumbled over a stone, and I caught him, his face inches from mine. He'd smiled, his features suddenly beautiful to me, and touched my cheek.

"You're so very wonderful, Jean. I'd be lost without you."

His eyes had been filled with so much affection, his smile warm. The thought of someone hurting him enraged me, and in that instant, I knew I loved him. He was mine, and no one would lay a hand on him. He'd changed my life. Changed *me*. If saving Alarick meant my end, I'd happily pay the price, knowing I'd lived a good life at his side.

"Jean." Alarick brought my hand between both of his, holding it tightly, his warmth flooding through me. "There's sadness in your smile. It breaks my heart to see you like this."

I tilted my head to one side. How was it possible he could be so insightful yet oblivious at the same time? He'd been doing this often lately, catching me off guard with tender words, expressing a deep concern for me, making certain I was all right. Even in the beginning, he'd been kind, never uttering a harsh word toward me. Ever so patient.

The room had gone quiet, and I lifted my head,

discreetly pulsing my magic to "see" where Sinopa had gone. She stood by the fireplace, her eyes on me, studying me before she turned her attention to Alarick.

"You really are concerned for Lord Eldrich, aren't you?"

"Of course I am," Alarick replied. "He's everything to me."

Sinopa gasped, and I shook my head in amusement. She took Alarick's words to mean more than what he intended. I was his companion, his friend. He loved me, told me as much often, but it wasn't the kind of love I had in my heart for him.

With a pat to my hand, Alarick stood and walked to the center of the room. "Where are we off to, then?"

"Scilla," I replied, standing.

Alarick sucked in a sharp breath. "I don't think that's a good idea. Perhaps we can search other avenues of gathering information?"

What wasn't he telling me? "We need someone who's been around as long as the scythe. Not to mention the scythe was originally lost somewhere in the Mediterranean Sea, which is Scylla's backyard." I folded my arms over my chest. "Alarick."

"The thing is, Scylla rather hates me."

"What did you do?"

"We were at a party together, and I might have had a bit too much wine one evening, flirted, one thing led to another —this was before we met, by the way."

I held back a smile, uncertain as to why he felt the need to tell me that, and motioned for him to continue.

"Anyway, I may have slipped out of her bed before dawn and not called her. In my defense, telephones hadn't been invented yet."

"Of course. Perfectly reasonable. Not as if you could

have sent word by any other means, what with you being the King of All Shifters."

He sighed. "I was a bit of a heartbreaker in my youth."

"Sounds to me like you were more of a cad."

Alarick gasped. "Jean!"

I couldn't hold back my laughter at his scandalized tone, especially as I suspected he sported a startled expression to match. "Goddess above, Alarick. How many of your exes are we in danger of encountering on this quest?"

"Oh, be quiet," he huffed.

My snort was most indelicate. "No, really."

"I don't know." He began to pace, and I could barely contain my laughter. "I've traveled all over the globe and have been alive since the beginning of time, Jean. A king has needs, you know."

Somewhere behind me, Sinopa let out a whispered, "Ew."

I nodded. "Right. Of course."

"I fell in with a rather questionable group of gods and nymphs during my youth. Zeus, especially, was a terrible influence."

Who did he think he was kidding? "Don't blame the gods for your dalliances."

"Very well. But at least *I* was single. I never cuckolded anyone." He nudged me with an elbow, and I just knew he'd winked at me. "Though I did do plenty of cock-holding."

"Oh dear Goddess!" My face went up in flames. "Go stand over there. Away from me. Perverted old man."

"Now see here, you're almost as old as I am. At least I think you are. You've never told me."

I scowled at him. "I'm far younger than you." Far. Far. *Far* younger.

"Really?"

"Yes." By two thousand years at least, but I wouldn't tell him so. He could be a little sensitive about his age at times.

"Perhaps it's because you're wise beyond your years."

"Mm, yes, must be that. Open the portal, Alarick."

Sinopa stepped up beside me, and I held back a smile.

"And where do you think you're going?" Alarick asked.

"With you. To help."

"It's far too dangerous. If something should happen to me—"

"Nothing will happen to you," I snapped. I would die before I let that bastard harm him.

Alarick laid a reassuring hand on my shoulder but continued to address Sinopa. "If something should happen to me, your citizens will need you. Please."

Sinopa was silent, but I could practically feel her seething. She wasn't about to accept standing on the sidelines. All of Alarick's shifter children were as stubborn as he was.

"Very well," she finally said. "I'll stay."

What was she up to? I remained silent on the matter. If Alarick wanted to believe Sinopa had merely agreed with him because he'd said so, he was fooling himself. He snapped his fingers and a portal appeared. Alarick stepped through first, and I was about to follow when Sinopa took hold of my sleeve, her soft voice filled with fear.

"Please, guard him well."

"With my life," I vowed. With a bow of my head, I ceased all use of my magic and stepped through the portal, the cool breeze from the sea misting my face. "Perhaps we should change out of our pajamas before we visit with your ex-girlfriend."

"She was never my girlfriend," Alarick protested before

snapping his fingers. At once I stood comfortably in one of my tailored suits. "Which colors did you choose?"

"Teal plaid for me, and royal blue for you."

"Wonderful. And here I was afraid you'd pick something conspicuous."

Alarick's boisterous laughter made it difficult to hold on to my frown. I loved the sound too much, loved the way it formed little creases at the corners of his eyes. My frown deepened. I missed not being able to call on my magic to see him and his smile. His arm around my waist startled me.

"Easy, Jean. It's me," he murmured softly.

That I knew. What I didn't know was why he had his arm around my waist. He drew me close and started leading me. Oh. Typically, Alarick led me with a hand to my elbow, or at most an arm around my shoulders.

"I want to keep you close," he informed me, his voice quiet in my ear.

The warmth of his breath on my skin and his lips brushing against my ear caused a shiver to go through me. I gritted my teeth. The hell with Nathair. If anyone was going to kill me, it would be Alarick with his blasted hot mouth and tender touches.

"Are you cold? I suppose it's a bit chilly here."

I hummed, neither confirming nor denying his assumption. This whole quest had me out of sorts. As if reading my thoughts, Alarick continued.

"You haven't been using your magic, so am I correct in assuming Nathair can somehow sense you when you use it?"

I couldn't help my surprise at how in tune he was with my thoughts. He must have noticed my expression.

"I may not know what manner of magical creature you are,

Jean, but I can feel your magic when you use it. Have felt it for as long as I've known you." The smile was evident in his tone, and it made me smile in return. He knew me so well. "Enjoy the walk," Alarick insisted. "It's a beautiful day. The sky is a brilliant blue, filled with wispy clouds, and the *Castello Ruffo di Calabria* still stands proudly on the promontory of Scilla."

The ancient fortification had been built on the southern shore of the Messina Strait, though we wouldn't be entering it to find Scylla. Instead we'd find her below it, inside the rocky cliff the castle had been built on.

Our shoes sank into the sand as we walked along the pebbled beach, the seagulls calling out to one another as they soared above our heads. The waves crashed against the shore, and I lifted my face to the heavens, smiling at the warmth of the sun against my skin. I was so lost in the peace that washed over me that I didn't realize Alarick had stopped walking. My cheeks warmed with embarrassment. I shouldn't have allowed myself to get distracted.

"Forgive me. I should be paying more attention," I told him, but received no reply. "Alarick?" Concerned, I turned to face him and reached out to touch him. He took my hand and placed it to his cheek. His soft hitch of breath caught my ear, and I tilted my head, my brows drawn together. "Are you all right?"

"Yes," he said quickly before clearing his throat. "It would seem I'm also guilty of being distracted. Let's get this over with, shall we? The sooner this mess is done with, the sooner we can go home. Perhaps when this is all over, I'll steal you away somewhere. How long has it been since we took a vacation?"

Firstly, he'd never stolen me anywhere. This was new. Secondly, Alarick didn't take vacations. As bold as he was, he preferred to remain in the comforts of his palace. "You want to go on vacation?"

"Remember when we used to travel all over the globe? Granted, it was often out of duty, but we still had a roaring good time, didn't we?"

"We did." Even if the trips had been part of his royal duty as king, we always managed to carve out some time to enjoy ourselves.

"I miss that," Alarick admitted quietly. "It's been too long."

I stopped and smiled at him. "Then we shall take a trip together once this is over."

"Just the two of us."

My heart skipped a beat. "I would love that." He looped his arm with mine, and we continued walking. A change in the scents around us made me still. I feared Nathair had found us, but as long as I didn't shift, he'd be forced to rely on other means of hunting us. That didn't mean we could become complacent. Nathair was crafty and resourceful. Relieved the scent I'd picked up wasn't his, we moved onward until we neared the Scillèo promontory.

"I wonder if this is what my children feel like when they embark on their quest?"

"How does it feel?"

Alarick seemed to consider my question. "Not pleasant."

"I imagine they feel slightly more terrified, considering the limited resources they're allowed for such a perilous journey and the fact most of them are sent off with a shifter unknown to them. It's no wonder they get so cross with you."

"The quests were your idea!"

"Hm. They were, weren't they?" I held back a smile. "But finding them a mate was yours."

Alarick let out a heavy sigh. "I just want them to be happy."

Whereas Alarick thought of his children's happiness and hearts, I had my own reasons for suggesting his royal shifter children prove themselves worthy of their crowns.

"Perhaps from now on you should inquire as to whether they desire a mate." As their king, Alarick could sense whether his children wished for a mate. He only had to send a whisper to them in their dreams. Unfortunately, Alarick believed himself all-knowing.

"Yes," Alarick muttered. "I've learned that lesson. I will ask from now on. You have my word."

"May I ask you a question?" The sand beneath my shoes turned into solid ground, and I felt the change around me. Alarick had pulled us into the magic realm.

"You know you can ask me anything, Jean."

"Why do you feel so strongly about finding them mates?"

Alarick stopped walking, and I felt his intense gaze on me. "Because they deserve to be loved."

I'd been unprepared for such a response. Alarick was a romantic at heart, always had been. Which was why it struck me as odd that he had never sought a mate for himself. As the King of All Shifters, and an immortal, finding the right mate would be a challenge, but not impossible. It was selfish of me, but I was grateful he'd not declared any interest in a mate. Just muttering the idea out loud would undoubtedly have our palace swarmed with potential candidates, including those seeking power.

"Don't you agree, Jean?"

Warmth flooded my entire body when he turned me to

face him. I placed my hands on his chest as he leaned his head closer to mine.

"We all deserve to be loved, don't we?" The words were almost a whisper, but I heard them down to the very depths of my soul.

What was happening? I lifted my head and leaned into him, his arms wrapped around me. He'd never held me this close before. "Alarick?" He tightened his hold, and my heart pounded in my ears. I could barely breathe. He was so close. His body was hard against mine, and although I'd seen him naked, had memorized every inch of his impressive body, having his muscular frame pressed to mine wreaked havoc with my senses. His scent enveloped me, a heady mixture of powerful shifter and the woodsy shower gel he loved.

Alarick and I were roughly the same height, but he was wider, with broad shoulders, his sturdy body tapering down to a slim waist. Everything about him exuded power, strength. Yet as he placed his fingers under my chin, his touch was feathery soft.

"Jean, I—"

"There you are. Took you long enough."

Startled, we jumped apart. I turned away from the two young shifters in an attempt to get myself under control. Goddess above, what was wrong with me? I was behaving like a lovesick fool, and Alarick... well, I had no idea what he was doing other than making me feel out of sorts. This behavior was so unlike him, and I was desperate to know the cause of this change.

"Prince Darton? Prince Seraphim? What are you two doing here?" Alarick asked, and I joined him in facing the two princes.

"We're here to keep you safe," the tallest of the two

princes proclaimed, shoulders rounded and chin lifted in regal fashion. My heart warmed. As Prince of the Deer Shifters, Prince Darton was tall, tawny-haired, and elegant, with warm brown eyes and a soft-spoken voice. He was kind and gentle, yet fierce when the time called for it. He was due to face his quest in just a few months. Beside him stood Prince Seraphim, Prince of the European Pine Marten Shifters, a tiny thing with near-black eyes, a sweet heart-shaped face, and pale blond hair that stood starkly against his bronzed skin tone. He was feisty, adventurous, and fearless.

Alarick stepped closer to me, his arm coming to rest around my shoulders. "How did you know we were here?"

"Princess Sinopa said someone is out to kill you," Darton replied worriedly.

Seraphim let out a little growl. "Not on our watch they won't." He really was quite adorable. Small in stature, as one expected from a Pine Marten shifter, but no less spirited than any of Alarick's shifter children. "Also, when am I getting my mate?"

"I have several candidates in mind," Alarick replied.

"I hope he's big. So I can climb him like a tree."

I couldn't help my laugh at the choked sound Alarick made in response. Seraphim's mate would certainly have his hands full. The shifter meant for him was not as big as Seraphim hoped for, but certainly bigger than him. Then again, most shifters were bigger than him. Seraphim in his Pine Marten form would be about the size of his mate's tail, if that.

It was an unlikely match, one I was quite certain Seraphim would curse Alarick over, but I'd already planted the seed in Alarick's mind, as I often did. Seraphim's mate would initially see him as prey, and Seraphim would see the red fox shifter as a threat. Neither had any notion of how much they needed each another.

"What's the plan?" Seraphim asked excitedly.

Alarick released a heavy sigh and guided me forward. "I don't suppose either of you will go home, even if I command it."

"Nope," Seraphim chirped as he hurried to keep up with us.

"You're our king," Darton offered gently. "We won't abandon you, no matter the danger."

Alarick sighed again. "Such stubborn children."

I chuckled. As if he'd expected any different. There was no getting rid of the two, and Alarick knew it.

"Very well, but stay close, and do as I say."

"Yes, Your Majesty," they replied in unison.

We headed toward the base of the castle, Seraphim to my right, and I assumed Darton to Alarick's left. When we reached what I believed to be the base of the rocky cliff, Alarick stopped. He stepped away from me, and the air changed around us. The soft breeze turned into a sharp, salty wind. The waves crashed violently against the shore, and a chilling roar echoed from somewhere inside the rock. Alarick returned to my side, his hand on my back as he led me forward.

The space before us became something new, and I discreetly sent a small pulse of magic around me in order to get a glimpse of where we now stood. I might have to rely on my other senses for a time, but I needed to remain vigilant. It was my duty to protect Alarick, and I would do so no matter the circumstances. Inside the cliff, hidden by magic, stood Scylla's grand Roman palace with its towering marble pillars, gilded archways, and ceilings covered in stunning art. It was striking and regal like the beautiful woman who approached, her skin milky white, hair like silk, and a face of pure sweetness. She smiled beautifully at me before her gaze moved to Alarick.

"Remain silent," I whispered hoarsely at him. "I'll do the talking."

"That's probably best," he muttered, taking a step behind me.

"Scylla, it's so wonderful to finally meet in person."

"Lord Eldrich," she said cheerfully, bringing me into a hug. "Such a pleasure. The tales don't do you justice."

"How very kind of you." I bowed my head over her hand and kissed it. "I'm afraid the stories are far more flattering than the reality."

Alarick sniffed. "Nonsense. You don't give yourself enough credit, Jean."

Despite his ignoring my insistence he remain quiet, I couldn't help my smile. He was always so quick to defend me.

Ever since my appearance at Alarick's side, countless tales had been spun in regard to my character and identity. The mystery surrounding me and my past had been the source of inspiration for many an outlandish tale. Some painted me as noble and heroic. Other stories proclaimed my ferocity and skills as a warrior. I never paid them much attention, but it would seem others did.

"Forgive us for arriving unannounced," I said with an apologetic bow.

"You are always welcome in my home, Lord Eldrich." Her smile faded when she once again moved her gaze to Alarick. "Unlike you."

"Come now, Scylla. You can't still be cross with me for not calling. It was such a long time ago. We were both young and frivolous. You don't look a day over two thousand, by the way."

Scylla hissed, and I elbowed Alarick in the ribs. Gods above, save me from this man's obtuseness.

Alarick leaned into me. "Is this another one of those apology things?"

"Yes, though I would advise you to consider your words *very* carefully. I have no desire to be turned into chum for her aquatic pets."

Alarick cleared his throat and took a step forward. "Scylla, I'd like to apologize for my awful behavior after our wonderful evening. We had a good time, didn't we? I know I did. Goddess, that thing you do with your tentacles—"

Sweet Aphrodite.

Scylla's shriek made the palace tremble. She threw her arms out, the wind howling as she expanded in size, tentacles exploding from her body, replacing her legs. About a dozen in total. Seraphim and Darton held on to me as six dog heads emerged from around her waist, snapping their fanged jaws. Scylla was a terrifying creature of legend, a beautiful nymph who'd been cursed and turned into a hideous sea monster that devoured sailors. At least that's who she'd been thousands of years ago. These days she tended to throw lavish parties filled with orgies, dancing, and drinking.

"Now, Scylla," Alarick cooed.

Oh dear Goddess. I grabbed Darton and Seraphim and quickly moved us away from Alarick just as Scylla lunged forward. She lashed out with one of her tentacles, and I winced as Alarick soared out of the palace. We ran outside in time to see the speck that was him off in the distance over the ocean. I covered my mouth with a fist to keep from barking out a laugh.

"Lord Eldrich?" Poor Darton sounded very concerned.

I waved a hand in dismissal. "He'll be fine. Give him a minute."

In the distance, something leapt through the water at great speeds. It went from a speck on the horizon to what was clearly a marlin, then a dolphin, then a very soaked Alarick dripping wet in front of us. Scylla shifted back into her human form and stepped up beside me, tittering joyously.

"Was that necessary?" Alarick sputtered as he wrung out his suit jacket, hair plastered to his face.

"No, but it was very entertaining. Come." Scylla spun on her heels and went inside.

As I turned, Alarick marched up beside me, growling, "This is your fault."

"My fault?"

"Yes! I apologized and was flung halfway across an ocean."

It was so very difficult not to laugh. "Well, technically you brought this on yourself."

"Can we get on with it?"

Scylla threw her head back and laughed. "Oh, Lord Eldrich, you *must* visit more often."

CHAPTER THREE

ALARICK

THIS WAS what I got for apologizing.

I removed my shoe, turned it upside down, and emptied it of the small ocean's worth of water inside. Ignoring Jean's laugh, I laid my shoe beside the other in front of the giant marble hearth and the warm roaring fire.

"You have more wrinkles," Scylla informed me.

"How very... unkind." I couldn't help my pout. There was no need for rudeness.

Scylla sighed and lifted my chin. "You know very well you're as handsome as ever. It's annoying."

I smiled brightly. "Thank you."

Her snort of disgust made me chuckle. She'd never admit it, but she liked me.

"Why are you here, Alarick?" She took a seat on her gold throne, crossing one long leg over the other, her flowing white dress hugging her ample curves.

Beautiful didn't do Scylla justice, but I no longer felt the pull toward her that I once had. These days my thoughts seemed occupied with someone a deal more... muscular. My gaze went to Jean, who stood quietly by the fire, Darton to his left and Seraphim to his right. They were here to guard me, yet they remained at his side, as if he offered them comfort or reassurance. Jean had that effect on my shifter children. Always had. They were drawn to him, often seeking him out for council. I couldn't blame them. He was extraordinary, in possession of a wit as sharp as his tongue. Jean would argue he wasn't charming, but he was. He had a way about him that confounded me yet drew me to him, as if I needed him at my side in order to breathe.

"Alarick?"

Snapping out of my thoughts, I smiled at Scylla. "It would seem you're not the only one I've vexed. Someone is out to kill me."

She rolled her eyes. "Who doesn't want to kill you?"

"Really?" I turned to Jean. "Why does everyone want to kill me?" This was certainly news to me. "Perhaps I should send out more holiday gift baskets."

"I doubt there are enough baskets in the world," Scylla muttered.

I arched an eyebrow at Jean, who merely shrugged, his lips pulled into a thin line like he was trying not to laugh. His smile faded as he turned to Scylla.

"Scylla, someone with the power to kill Alarick truly wishes him dead."

A small gasp escaped her, a hand going to her chest. "Oh." The concern in her was touching. "Alarick, this is terrible news."

"I knew you cared," I teased.

Scylla rolled her eyes at me again before leaving her

throne and stopping before me. "Alarick, if you are killed, the heavens will be off-balance and the gods will descend to Earth, throwing the world into chaos. Few will survive."

There was that.

She narrowed her gaze at me. "You don't seem overly concerned."

"Would it make you feel better if I ran around in a panic and aimlessly flailed my arms?" I made to throw up my arms, but Jean caught them with a sigh.

"Let's not," he murmured. "Scylla, there is only one weapon capable of defeating the assassin out to kill Alarick."

Scylla didn't miss a beat. "The Scythe of Kronos."

"Yes. We were hoping you might know where it is."

"I'm afraid the scythe disappeared from my ocean thousands of years ago. It's almost impossible to trace."

"Why is that?" Seraphim asked. "I mean, it looks like a scythe, right? Can't we just get word out to all our shifter siblings and ask them to look for a magical scythe?"

Jean shook his head. "The scythe becomes whatever weapon is needed for the holder to defeat their enemy."

"It can turn into anything?" Darton asked.

Jean nodded. "Exactly."

"Well, that stinks." Seraphim threw up his arms. "How are we supposed to find a weapon that can literally be anything?"

Scylla tapped a red nail against her chin. "I do know of one who might have the information you seek."

"Would you be a dear?" I pointed to my wet clothes. Normally, Jean would have dried me, but he was attempting to keep his powers hidden from Nathair, and out of respect for Scylla, I asked her instead of using my magic. She snapped her fingers, and once again I was warm and bliss-fully dry.

"Who?" Jean asked as he fixed my shirt collar, then brushed a curl away from my brow. Ever so attentive. I'd grown so used to having his hands on me.

Scylla's evil grin didn't bode well. "His name is Ziv."

I groaned, and Jean spun to face me.

"Let me guess. He's not fond of you either?"

"More like loathes him," Scylla replied, far too happy about the fact.

"So much hostility."

Jean gaped at me. "Another one of your exes?"

"It's a long story."

"I'm certain it is," Jean muttered, arms crossed over his chest. "Where can we find Ziv?"

"Lérins Islands on the Côte d'Azur," I replied. "In the forests of Île Sainte-Marguerite, to be exact."

"Wonderful." Jean turned to Scylla and bowed grace-fully. "Thank you for your help, Scylla. It was a pleasure to see you."

"The pleasure was mine, Lord Eldrich." She kissed Jean's cheek and turned to me with a sweet smile. "Alarick. Try not to die."

"Um, thank you?"

"I didn't know you had pet snakes," Seraphim said, pupils dilating. He looked about ready to pounce on any one of the half a dozen snakes slithering out from the walls.

Scylla wrinkled her nose as she shooed one of the snakes away. "I live in a cliff by the sea. Something is always making its way in. Good luck on your journey."

"Thank you for not tearing me limb from limb," I said brightly, chuckling when she grunted in response. With a snap of my fingers, I opened up three portals, one to Île

Sainte-Marguerite for Jean and myself, one for Darton, and one for Seraphim. "You kept us safe. Now it's time for you two to go home."

The two young shifters exchanged glances before turning their attention back to me, deep frowns on their sweet faces. Seraphim was the first to speak up.

"Your Majesty, please. We want to help."

"And I appreciate it, I do. But there's no need. Jean and I will be just fine." I motioned for them to go on, and after some hesitation, Seraphim let out a heavy sigh, then disappeared through his portal.

"Be careful," Darton pleaded before disappearing as well.

With a final wave at Scylla, Jean and I stepped through our portal, appearing in a lush forest filled with towering trees, the sun's rays shining through the thick greenery. I waved a hand and the magic realm engulfed us, otherworldly flowers now visible, enchanted birds chirping from numerous tree branches high above our heads while fairies darted from place to place. The world around us grew brighter, more colorful. A soft breeze caressed my cheek, carrying a familiar scent.

Ziv leapt from behind several trees, a huge stag with the hind legs, tail, and wings of a peacock. He fanned out his tail, wings spread as he pranced toward us. A truly magnificent creature. Perytons were rare these days. Sadly, Ziv had lost many of his kind over the years to hunters and poachers from the magic realm.

"That's Ziv?" Jean asked, sounding surprised.

"Yes."

"He's... stunning."

Jean's tone caught my attention, and I turned, frowning at the concern etched onto his handsome face.

"What's wrong?"

Jean shook his head. He was attempting to keep his magic use to quick tiny pulses and therefore couldn't see me, yet he refused to face me. It was unlike Jean to look so... uncertain.

"Jean?"

A sad smile came onto his lips. "It's nothing. I'm being silly."

I was certain he wasn't. Silly was not a word anyone associated with Jean. Something was bothering him. A huff made me turn toward Ziv, and for a heartbeat, I considered whether Jean was comparing himself to the elegant Peryton, who was as impressive in his magical beast form as he was in his human one. Ziv was a stunning creature, but if I had to choose, no question Jean would win every time. The thought took me by surprise. I had no idea what manner of creature Jean was, and yet I couldn't imagine anyone being more beautiful than him. Not thinking, I leaned in to kiss his cheek.

"No one can hold a candle to you, Jean. Not even Ziv."

Jean gasped, his cheeks turning a lovely shade of pink. "Alarick—"

"Well, look who it is." Ziv stopped several feet away from us, arms crossed over his slender chest. He was all long legs and smooth tanned skin. He had the body of a ballet dancer and moved with the grace of one. His sandy-blond hair fell roguishly over one eye, his plump pink lips pursed as he looked me over. His tongue poked out to run across his bottom lip before he moved closer, big silver eyes fixed on my face.

"Ziv, how lovely to see you."

Ziv smiled sweetly as he stepped up to me. "Hello, handsome."

The sting left on my cheek after he slapped me was rather impressive.

"How dare you!" Jean lunged forward, and I threw my arms around him, relieved I was quick enough. Few could match Jean's speed when he leapt into action.

"Give us a moment, won't you?" I pulled Jean to one side. "What's come over you?"

"How dare he lay a hand on you! I should pluck him where he stands." Jean was all but vibrating with anger. I'd never seen him like this. Goddess above, it was exhilarating. Quickly I pushed that outrageous thought aside. Jean wouldn't hesitate to put Ziv in his place, and we needed answers from him first. Wait. Was Jean... jealous?

"Are you jealous?"

"What? Don't be absurd. Jealousy is a sentiment for small-minded fools."

"You *are* jealous." I stared at him, astonished.

"I am not," he replied through his teeth. "I would never be jealous of such a pompous, overdressed jackalope with chicken legs."

"What did he call me?" Ziv growled from behind us.

Oh no. This was very bad. I feared this situation was on the verge of spiraling out of my control. "Jean, please. We need him to help us find the scythe before Nathair finds us."

Jean's nostrils flared, but he nodded, his lips pressed together in a thin line. He stepped around me and bowed to Ziv. "Forgive me for my shameful behavior."

Ziv eyed Jean warily before moving his gaze to me. "What's with the bandage around his eyes? Who is he?"

"He is Lord Eldrich. Jean, this is Ziv."

Jean bowed his head again. "Again, I apologize for my behavior."

"Sure," Ziv replied. "Wait, *the* Lord Eldrich?" He

moved his gaze back to me. "*He's* the one everyone's so terrified of?"

I beamed at Ziv. "Oh yes, and his reputation is well deserved. Jean is a most formidable warrior. He's protected me for thousands of years."

"But..." Ziv shook his head, puzzled. "He's blind."

"I may be blind, but I can hear just fine," Jean growled. He did not like Ziv at all, and I couldn't blame him. Ziv might be wild in bed, but he could be rather arrogant and self-absorbed. Jean muttered something under his breath about not needing his sight to see Ziv was an ass. I coughed into my hand in an attempt to stifle my laughter. Ziv cocked his head to one side, his eyes narrowed at Jean.

Ziv became nothing but a blur of color, moving at a speed undetectable to humans. I'd not expected the attack, but I didn't need to. In the blink of an eye, Jean stood before me, his body shielding mine, one hand wrapped around Ziv's wrist, keeping the blade he wielded away from my throat. Ziv stared at Jean, eyes huge.

Jean appeared unmoving, his voice low and filled with warning when he spoke. "The only reason you're not on the ground drowning in a pool of your own blood is because we need answers."

Goodness, that escalated quickly.

Ziv jerked his arm away. He opened his hand and the blade disappeared. "Such a loyal beast."

"Watch your words, Ziv," I warned, the forest growing dark as a storm rolled in from the sea, a thick fog moving through the trees. Lightning crackled around me, the wind picked up, and my eyes flashed as I summoned my powers. "You will show him respect." My voice sounded as if it weren't my own, connected to the heavens above us.

Ziv took a quick step back, his body trembling with fear.

"Alarick, that's not necessary," Jean murmured in my ear, his fingers caressing my jaw as he soothed me. "Rein in your power, my king."

All at once, the skies cleared and the sun returned. I smiled warmly at Jean. "You're wonderful," I told him. "And so very good for me." Once I'd matured, while the deities around me were all about inflicting their wrath, I was lulled into pleasurable bliss by the simple act of laying my head on Jean's lap after a difficult day. I couldn't imagine the manner of king I would have become without him.

Jean laughed softly. "Someone has to keep you out of trouble."

"I'm so very glad it's you." Taking his hand in mine, I lifted his fingers to my lips and kissed them. I couldn't explain why I did such a thing, only that the urge to do so had overwhelmed me. It felt right, his hand in mine. I turned my attention back to Ziv. "Why are you staring at me like that?"

Ziv shook his head, seeming to snap out of it. "Sorry, I've never seen you like this."

"Jean is very dear to me. A slight against him is a slight against me."

Jean squeezed my arm. "Is this true?"

"Of course," I replied with a sniff. "When have I ever allowed anyone to disrespect you?" I thought back over our time together. "Granted, anyone who insulted you tended to meet a swift demise shortly after." Those who'd been bold enough to insult Jean were usually out to harm one of us. It had been quite some time since someone had the power to threaten my life.

"You both are so very strange," Ziv muttered. He crossed his arms over his chest. "What do you want, Alarick?"

I opened my mouth to reply, but three portals appeared to my right. Beside me, Jean laughed quietly as I released a heavy sigh.

"Stubborn, aren't they?" I muttered.

"They're *your* children," Jean replied with a snicker.

"I feel as though when they're being this stubborn, they should be *your* children."

Jean let out a bark of laughter, and I held back a smile as I turned to the two princesses and one prince. I wasn't about to think further on how much I liked the idea of Jean sharing some of the parental responsibilities with me.

"Let me guess," I said, folding my arms over my chest as I narrowed my gaze at them. "Princess Sinopa sent you to protect me."

Gavina, Princess of the Hawk Shifters, stepped forward, her near-black eyes intense as she met my stare. "She warned us you'd be uncooperative."

"We're not leaving," Sova pitched in. As Princess of the Little Owl Shifters, she was a tiny thing with big yellow eyes, and I just wanted to scoop her up and squeeze her because she was so cute! Her scowl was fierce. Or so she believed, I'm certain. I moved my gaze to Prince Leveret, Prince of the European Hare Shifters. He stood tall and elegant, a handsome young shifter with an athletic build and long legs.

"Where's Haider?" I asked Leveret. "I'm surprised your mate has let you out of his sight."

Leveret's cheeks turned a bright pink as he brushed his honey-blond hair away from his face. Newly mated, Leveret and his lion shifter mate, Haider, were inseparable. I'd been a little concerned about the match, considering how different the two were. Haider was older, a fierce warrior who'd seen many a battle, but Jean had chosen well, always did. The mostly silent soldier took one look at the pretty hare prince and melted. Leveret struggled with the idea of a lion as his mate at first, but he could only fight his heart so long.

"He wasn't happy about staying behind," Levert admitted. "But he's on standby should we need the backup."

"Alarick? What's going on?" Ziv took a step forward, and Jean stepped closer to me, stopping Ziv from advancing any farther. "Surely your shifter children aren't showing up to protect you from *me*."

Jean scoffed. "Don't be ridiculous. We're here due to a real threat."

I cringed, dropping my gaze in the hopes of averting Ziv's fierce glare. In all the years I'd known Jean, I'd never seen him behave in such a fashion toward anyone. Ziv wasn't the first handsome creature we'd faced, yet Jean seemed particularly disgruntled by his presence. Best I hurry things along and put an end to this encounter, for all our sakes.

"Ziv, I was hoping you might know the whereabouts of a certain godly weapon. The Scythe of Kronos."

A gasp escaped Ziv, his eyes filled with concern, and he ignored Jean's growl, hurrying over to me. "Goddess above, Alarick. What have you gotten yourself into?"

"Nothing you need to concern yourself with, but it's imperative I locate the scythe."

Ziv seemed to consider my words. He didn't look very happy about the prospect, but I was grateful when he didn't ask any further questions. "I haven't seen the scythe in over a thousand years, but I know someone who's seen it far more recently. He's rather difficult to find these days, but if you can track him down, he should be able to get you a solid lead."

"Who?" Jean asked.

"The Alpha of the Cù-Sìth."

I turned to Jean. "Do you think it's possible?"

Jean sighed. "Knowing you, it most likely is."

"What are you talking about?" Gavina asked, looking from me to Jean and back.

"I think I know someone who can find the Alpha of the Cù-Sìth. They met during a quest, though he didn't know the hound they'd spoken with was alpha." I turned to open several portals and instruct my children to go home, when the air changed, a putrid smell filling my nostrils.

Jean threw his arms out, an intricately designed medieval spear axe appearing in each hand. No one was as skilled as Jean when it came to the art of dual-weapon combat. It had been so long since I'd seen him wield such weapons.

"The portals, Alarick!"

I opened the portals just as the forest around us filled with battle cries. Beasts I had not seen since the dawn of time lunged from behind the trees, wielding swords. Half man, half snake, killers from an ancient world. Nathair had found some recruits. We needed to move fast. If Nathair's followers had found us, it wouldn't be long before Nathair himself arrived, especially with Jean having to use his powers.

With a battle cry, Jean launched into the fray. I snapped my fingers, arming my shifter children with swords before arming myself. The beasts snarled as they coiled and leapt into attack. Jean showed no mercy, his spear axes making quick work of our enemies. I wasn't overly concerned about myself. These creatures could not kill me, and neither could their weapons. However, I took great offense at their putting my shifter children in harm's way.

Since it was me they wished dead, I stood patiently, waiting for them to come to me. I didn't need to wait long. The more Jean dispatched, the more appeared. A horde of at least half a dozen or so charged me. I sent a pulse of magic at them with my free hand that knocked them off their tails. They quickly slithered upright.

"I'm giving you the chance to walk away... er, slither away, or you shall meet the fate of your brethren."

"Nathair sends his regards," one hissed.

"That makes no sense. Why do lackeys always say that? Who sends terrible regards? No one, that's who. Unless he's sending me kind regards, which is doubtful." Two lunged at me, and I grasped the handle of my sword with both hands, reached back, and sliced through the air, the blade of my sword extending and slicing through the two beasts like silk. Not waiting for the others to leap at me, I jabbed and swung, spun on my heels, and lashed back, taking several down at once. I ducked beneath a blade, swinging my sword with me as I rose, ridding myself of one more adversary.

My eyes and nose burned from the smell of putrid rot left behind by their blood, and around me the sound of steel clashing against steel reminded me of the battles I'd fought in my youth.

"Leveret!"

I spun at Gavina's shout in time to see two serpent beasts lunge at Leveret, knocking him to the ground. With a snarl I advanced, my speed matched only by Jean's. We reached Leveret, our swords meeting that of the attackers before they could strike. Quicker than a heartbeat, Jean sliced through both of the slithering bastards. I reached down and pulled Leveret to his feet.

"Are you all right?"

He nodded, his chest rising and falling with rapid pants. "Thank you."

Jean turned to rid us of another one of the creatures, and Leveret's eyes widened, his gaze behind me. He lifted his sword and shouted my name as the beast's sword struck a blow against my back. I turned and arched an eyebrow at the now stunned creature. It looked from its sword to me and back.

"Hello," I said, waving cheerfully. "King Alarick, King of All Shifters. Immortal. Your weapons can't hurt me."

Its eyes widened before it fell in two pieces on the ground before me. Jean stepped over it and fussed at me. So sweet.

"Are you all right? Did he hurt you?"

I cupped his cheek. "You know he didn't."

Jean hissed in anger. "Nathair will regret this day."

"Alarick!" Ziv came running, eyes wide. "There's an entire army of the beasts heading this way."

"Run!" I demanded of the three young shifters as I opened portals to their realms. I'd not allow them to be harmed. The three glared at me before Leveret thrust his sword into the air.

"Protect the king!"

"Oh, for crying out loud." I spun to Jean, who shrugged, the smile on his face not helping at all. "Enough of this." I called the power of the heavens down to me, lightning splitting the now darkened skies as the earth trembled beneath our feet. My sword vanished as I reached up toward the sky, my sight growing sharp as my body began to glow. "Everyone, close your eyes *now*!"

The serpent beasts broke through the trees just as I clapped my hands together, the blast of light exploding from me as bright as a supernova. It swept across the forest, disintegrating the monsters. Portals opened, and more creatures emerged. I turned to my shifter children, reached out a hand, and swept them up, tossing each one into their respective open portal.

"Time to go home, and thank you!" I closed the portals before they could attempt to return, then turned to Ziv, who'd shifted. "Thank you for your help. Stay safe." He bowed his regal head before taking off into the sky. "Let's go, Jean. This forest has gotten a little crowded. Grabbing his hand, I opened a portal and quickly closed it the moment we'd stepped through. "Well, that was invigorating."

Jean shook his head at me, his lips quirked in a smile. "Come. Let's find our favorite feisty feline."

Oh, this was going to be interesting.

CHAPTER FOUR

JEAN

Nᴀᴛʜᴀɪʀ ᴇᴅɢᴇᴅ ᴇᴠᴇʀ ᴄʟᴏsᴇʀ.

I refrained from using more than a subtle pulse of magic, mostly relying on my heightened senses to pick up the familiar scents and sounds of the palace around us. I inhaled a deep breath, enjoying the fragrance of flowers and the subtle whiff of freshly baked bread. The light from the row of windows along the corridor offered a cheerful brightness equal to the nature of its inhabitants. In the distance I heard the happy chatter of palace staff as they went about their duties. We were safe. For now.

We needed to find that blasted scythe. It was merely a matter of time before Nathair appeared, and I had no doubt his minions weren't far. Thankfully, Nathair could only summon a portal if I used my magic while entering one, and I didn't have the power to summon portals, but Alarick and his shifter princes and princesses did. This alone kept

Nathair a step behind us. Knowing this, he hadn't waited long to align himself with creatures of dark magic. Who knew what else lay in wait for us out there?

A familiar scent filled the air, and I smiled as the wolf shifter rounded the corner, heading toward us. "Grimm, forgive us for visiting unannounced. I hope you're well."

"Lord Eldrich, Your Majesty, it's always a pleasure to see you. And I'm very well. Thank you." Grimmwolf stood tall, a handsome wolf shifter with silver hair, sparkling gray eyes, and a bright smile. He was dressed all in gray, from his boots and pants to his soft gray sweater. An alpha wolf, and next in line to be Prince of the Wolf Shifters, Grimm was kind yet powerful. He'd been an excellent match for Prince Owin, despite the two getting off to a rough start.

"How may I be of service?" Grimm asked, with a deep bow.

"Where is your mate?" I asked, catching Prince Owin's scent nearby.

"Attending to his royal duties. He'll be along any moment."

Alarick took hold of my elbow, and I followed him as Grimm led us somewhere we might speak in private. "He's not still cross with me, is he?" Alarick gently moved me in front of him to enter the room. Once inside, I sent out a steady stream of tiny pulses so I could see.

At no point during our time together had I asked Alarick to become my guide when I couldn't use my magic, but there had been no need. He'd simply fallen into the habit without prompting. Over the course of our friendship, Alarick often showed his affection in little ways. Most of the time, he had no idea he was even doing it. It made my heart soar.

"Oh, do you mean is he still cross at you for allowing

him to believe you were going to have me dragged to the fae underworld?" Grimm waved a hand, his gray eyes alight with amusement. "Nah."

I couldn't help my grin. I had a feeling Grimm wasn't being entirely honest with Alarick. Felines were exceptionally good at holding grudges. They simply bided their time, striking with mighty vengeance when least expected. As the ocelot shifter prince, Owin was small but fierce. His tiny teeth were quite stabby, especially if he got ahold of your ankles.

"Perhaps we should get to the reason we're here," Alarick muttered.

I brought Grimm up to speed regarding Nathair and his quest to kill Alarick. Gimm stood dumbstruck as the room plunged into silence. Then, seeming to shake himself out of it, Grimm stepped forward, his hands balled into fists at his side.

"And you need me to join the fight?"

Alarick cleared his throat. "No. Um, we need you to—"

A hiss met my ears, and I dropped my gaze to find the little ocelot prince latched on to Alarick's shoe, back paws kicking as he sank his sharp tiny teeth into the leather. I glanced at Grimm, who shrugged, his lips quirked in a smile.

"Still sore at me, are you?" Alarick asked Owin, who kicked at his shoe a few more times for good measure before releasing him. He hissed at Alarick, his back arched as he jumped sideways toward his mate, fur bristled.

I often referred to Alarick's shifter children as divas, and Owin was at the top of the list. Yet despite his temper, he was sweet and good. He might be smaller than his alpha wolf mate, but no one defended Grimm like the young prince.

Grimm lowered to one knee. "Come now, love. The king needs my help. You can unleash your vengeance upon him at a later date. I'm sure Lord Eldrich can pencil you in."

I coughed into my hand in the hopes of holding back my laughter. Alarick rolled his eyes and smiled at Owin, who shifted, his amber eyes narrowed at Alarick. He wrapped his arms around Grimm's waist, as if he could protect his mate from our king.

"Your Majesty," Owin grumbled by way of greeting before moving his gaze to me, a smile lighting up his boyish features. "Lord Eldrich, how nice to see you!"

"Really?" Alarick huffed, grumbling something under his breath. He winked at me to let me know he wasn't actually upset.

"Wait." Owin turned and lifted his gaze to Grimm's. "You said the king needs your help. What's going on?"

Alarick seemed to be bracing himself. "We need Grimm to take us to the Cù-Sìth."

"What? Why can't you simply portal there yourself?"

"The Cù-Sìth that Grimm took you to see during your quest happens to be the Alpha of the Cù-Sìth," I explained. "Just as your quest took you to the Hellhound alpha."

Owin frowned up at Grimm. "Did you know that?"

Grimm shook his head and shrugged. "I simply asked the magic satchel to take us to whoever we needed to see."

"And it did," I said with a smile. "As you are of alpha blood, it took you to someone of equal standing. The Cù-Sìth are connected to the fae, and you know how... *challenging* it is to deal with them. Grimm, you're a canine, as is the Cù-Sìth. Distant cousins, if you will. There's less chance we'll be dragged to the fae underworld if you initiate the meeting."

"Wait." Owin held up a hand, eyes blazing. "Are you

saying when we met him there had been a chance he'd take us both to the fae underworld?"

"No, I'd worked out an agreement for that occasion," I replied. "But the Cù-Sìth are unpredictable. There's no telling how they would react to Alarick and I in their land."

"Absolutely not!"

"Owin..." Grimm attempted to soothe his mate, but Owin was having none of it.

"No! I won't risk losing you."

"If I don't do this, our king could die."

Owin stared up at Grimm, eyes wide. "What?"

Grimm brought Owin into his arms. The young prince melted against Grimm, releasing a little sigh. When Grimm pulled back, Owin's cheeks were flushed. With Owin in a calm state, Grimm filled him in on the situation with Nathair. "Love, think of what would happen to our world, to our citizens, if the King of All Shifters was killed."

Owin rested his brow against Grimm's chest, his fingers tightening on Grimm's sleeves. He nodded, then lifted his gaze to Alarick.

"I understand. I'm coming with you." Before Grimm could protest, Owin held up a hand. "No. My mate and I will accompany you together or not at all."

Alarick turned to me, and I sighed. Surely somewhere out there Alarick had a shifter child who wasn't so damned headstrong. "Very well. But at the first sign of trouble, I want you both back here." The likelihood they'd listen was slim, but I liked to fool myself every once in a while and pretend these youngsters might do as they were told.

"Of course," Owin said before turning to Grimm. "We should get your magic purse."

"Satchel," Grimm corrected with a kiss to the tip of Owin's nose.

"No need," Alarick informed them and snapped his fingers. The enchanted satchel he'd gifted Grimm appeared, slung around Grimm's torso.

Owin straightened his cute little blue bow tie. "Where are we off to, then?"

"Inchcailloch Island," Alarick replied.

"All right. Here goes everything." Grimm reached into the satchel and removed a glowing orb. When he tossed it onto the floor, it stretched into a doorway, and on the other side a gorgeous forest appeared, with touches of bright pinks and purples, a carpet of bluebells, and the twinkling lights of faeries darting here and there. I took one last look before ceasing all use of my magic.

"Ready?" Alarick asked me.

I nodded, smiling when he took my hand in his, our fingers laced together. My heart leapt into my throat as he brought me close to him as we crossed the threshold deep into the woods. Birds chirped, a soft breeze ruffled my hair, and the sound of water lapping nearby caught my ear. The satchel's portal brought us straight into the magic realm, but then I assumed wherever the Alpha of the Cù-Sìth stepped, the magic realm surrounded him.

"What now?" Owin asked quietly.

"Now we wait," I said. "He will find us."

"It's so beautiful here," Alarick said wistfully, and I tilted my head in question. "We've been so busy lately with all the quests, we haven't taken any time for us, have we?"

"Us?" His words both startled me and sent my pulse soaring.

"Walk with me."

"But the Cù-Sìth?"

"We won't wander far," Alarick promised.

"It's fine," Grimm assured us. "We'll be right here."

Alarick gently pulled me with him, and I realized then that he hadn't released my hand. We treaded carefully through the lush greenery, and in my mind's eye I could see the flowers glowing bright. They gave off the most wonderful scent. I lifted my face to the skies, felt the flickering warmth from the sunshine cutting through the towering trees.

"Can you hear that?" I asked him, my smile stretched wide.

"Hear what?"

"Celtic music." It was faint, but I heard it clear as day.

"I don't hear anything, but then I suppose if someone is going to hear the magic of the fae, it would be you."

"Oh?"

Alarick turned to face me, his body close to mine as he cupped my cheek. "May I say something bold, Jean?"

I nodded.

Alarick seemed to hesitate. "Perhaps I shouldn't. You're my dearest friend, and I would never forgive myself if my actions caused me to lose you." He made to step away, but I held on to the lapels of his suit jacket.

"No, please." I'd never begged before, but it slipped out of me, surprising me, and from his soft gasp, him too. "You could never lose me, Alarick. Say whatever is on your mind."

"Very well." He stroked my cheek with his thumb and leaned his head closer to mine. "I... I feel as though I might be going mad."

"What do you mean?"

"For some time now, I've been thinking... certain things about you. Things I had never considered in all our years of friendship."

"Like what?" I asked, holding my breath. I itched to use

my magic, to see his face, his beautiful eyes swirling with power. Heat rolled off his body, his arm coming around my waist and squeezing me.

Alarick ran his fingers through my hair, the smile evident in his voice when he spoke. "Like wondering what it would feel like to run my fingers through your hair. How handsome you are, how strong..."

My cheeks heated. Never would I have believed he'd had such thoughts about me. I leaned into his touch, letting out a soft sigh at the feel of his hand in my hair. Love was not a sentiment I'd been born to feel, yet it had grown inside me from being near this amazing creature.

"I've had... thoughts of you." He cleared his throat. "Terribly naughty thoughts."

My smile turned wicked. "Oh? Would you care to share them?" I reached up, and he took my hand, placing it to his cheek. Giving in to my urges, I placed my thumb over his bottom lip, and he nipped at it, making me gasp.

"I would rather show you."

My heart threatened to beat out of me. Had Alarick just said what I thought he had? I stilled, my heart pounding fiercely as he placed his fingers under my chin and lifted my face, his warm breath caressing my skin as his lips brushed over mine. I had dreamed of this day for so very long. To feel his lush lips on mine, to know his taste. I yearned for him with a burning desire I'd never imagined.

"Your Majesty! Lord Eldrich!"

I was going to murder someone.

My growl made Alarick chuckle, and I contemplated whether *he* would be the one I dispatched. Goddess above, my heart couldn't take much more of this. We hurried back to where we'd left Owin and Grimm, the scent of wet grass and hound hitting my nostrils. The Alpha of the Cù-Sìth had arrived.

"Grimmwolf. Good thing I recognized yer scent. I was about to drag ye all off to the underworld," the Alpha of the Cù-Sìth said in his thick brogue.

"That would have been awkward," Alarick replied with a warm laugh. He bowed regally. "Greetings, Alpha."

The Alpha of the Cù-Sìth nodded a greeting in return, his eyes narrowed in suspicion.

"How have you been?" Grimm asked, returning the alpha's attention to him.

"Ah, ye know how it is. Work, work, work. So many souls to deliver, so little time. How can I help ye?"

"We have a bit of a crisis on our hands, and we need to locate the Scythe of Kronos."

"The Scythe of Kronos?"

The Cù-Sìth's stunned tone was expected. I doubted anyone had come looking for such a weapon in a very long time.

"What would ye need a weapon like that fer?"

Owin stepped forward. "An ancient evil has risen to destroy King Alarick, and he has the power to do so. The ancient gods will descend from the heavens and throw our world into darkness! Think of all the chaos! So much chaos!"

So dramatic, our little ocelot prince.

"Chaos, ay? That sounds terrible," the Cù-Sìth replied calmly.

"It's more than terrible! It's terrifying! All those hotheaded gods that can't seem to keep it in their pants descending to Earth," Owin cried, followed by a sharp meow.

"And he shifted," Alarick murmured beside me. "He scares himself quite easily, doesn't he?"

"Owin, sweetheart," Grimm cooed, then hissed. My guess was his ocelot mate was climbing him as if he were a tall tree. "Ouch! Watch where you stick those claws, love. They're tiny but razor-sharp."

The Cù-Sìth let out a booming laugh. "I'll help ye. Only because your little feline mate is quite entertaining."

Another meow and hiss met my ear, but the Cù-Sìth alpha simply laughed.

"So much spirit for something so small."

Alarick wrapped his arm around my waist, and we started moving, following the alpha through the woods.

"You know where it is, then?" Alarick asked just as Grimm sucked in a sharp breath. Owin had undoubtedly clawed him again.

"Yer in luck. My clan has kept it hidden for many a century. It fell into human hands a few decades ago, but my hounds managed to retrieve it. Goddess knows, humans are the last creatures who should be in possession of such a weapon." The Cù-Sìth alpha stopped, and I felt his gaze on us. "I expect ye'll be returning it to me once ye've finished with it."

It wasn't a question. "Absolutely," I replied. "It's best you keep it hidden and safe from everyone."

Seeming satisfied with my response, he started walking again. The breeze became cooler as we drew closer to the loch, the faint sound of water gently lapping against the shore growing louder. We stopped, and I faced the loch.

"It's buried at the bottom of the loch, isn't it?"

"Of course it is," Owin grumbled. "Do you know where at the bottom of the loch?"

"Sorry, no."

"It's fine," Alarick said, turning to face me and resting his hand on the side of my neck. I leaned into the touch and covered his hand with mine. "I'll be back shortly. Should anything occur while I'm searching, you take the children and run."

I arched an eyebrow at him, making him laugh softly.

"Fine, but at least stay safe."

That I could promise. I nodded, and he was off, a splash of water the only indication he'd shifted and dove in. I sniffed the air, smiling as Owin stepped up beside me.

"So... you and King Alarick, huh?"

"What about us?"

"I've never seen him all soft and touchy-feely with you. Well, he's always been rather hands-on with you, but this time it seemed different. I always wondered if you two were—"

"We're not," I said quickly. Perhaps a bit too quickly.

Owin hummed. "Lord Eldrich, it may have taken almost losing Grimm to realize how much I loved him, but anyone who spends any time around the two of you can see how deeply the king cares for you."

"I've been his companion for thousands of years. He's my dearest friend."

"I hate to break it to you, but friends don't stare dreamily at each other and touch the way you both do."

My cheeks were suddenly feeling a bit warm. How was I being schooled in matters of the heart by one of Alarick's children?

"It's all right. You don't have to discuss it."

"Good. I wasn't planning to." I folded my arms over my chest, enjoying the cool spring breeze. From what I remembered, the loch was rather grand in size. What if Alarick couldn't find it? No, I had faith in him. If anyone could find it, Alarick could.

"Personally, I think it's about time."

I turned in the direction of Grimm's voice, my brows drawn together. "About time for what?"

"For the king to find his mate."

I gaped at Grimm. "Mate?"

"Ya know, you two aren't getting any younger," the Cù-Sìth pitched in.

What was happening right now? "I am not discussing my love life or lack thereof with any of you. Can we please focus on finding the one weapon capable of keeping the world from plunging into a terrifying chaotic nightmare?"

"Are ye not interested in becoming mate to the King of All Shifters?" the Cù-Sìth asked.

"I will not dignify such a question with a response." How I felt about Alarick was no one's business but my own.

"He's sort of... handsome, I suppose," Owin mused. "For an old, *old* guy."

"He's not old, he's immortal," I snapped. "And he's very handsome. Exceptionally handsome."

"He's a little odd," Grimm added.

"He's charming," I corrected with a sniff.

"Kind of oblivious at times," Owin said cheerfully.

"He's wonderful," I replied through my teeth. "If you knew him as I did, you would know he's kind, gentle, sweet, and funny. He is far smarter than he's given credit for, not to mention he would lay down his life for any of his shifter children. We could not have been blessed with a greater king. Anyone worthy enough to be chosen as his mate would kneel before him in gratitude."

Owin snickered, and I narrowed my eyes at him. Not that he could see them from behind my bandage.

"Would you do that for me, Jean?"

My gasp was loud even to my own ears as I jumped higher than a certain startled ocelot. "Alarick!" Those sneaky little bastards. Wait. "How long have you been standing there?" Alarick stepped in front of me, and I reached out to touch his chest. "You're soaking wet."

"I was at the bottom of a lake," he said, a rumble of a chuckle rising from his broad chest. He leaned his head close to mine. "Well, Jean, would you?"

"Would I what?" He was so close, his body warm despite his soaked clothes.

"Get down on your knees for me?"

I swallowed thickly. *Yes. A thousand times, yes. I would do anything for you.* "Oh, um, I…" His lips brushed mine, and I melted against him. "What was the question?" This was so very infuriating. I was a deadly warrior, a former assassin, but at this moment with his arms around me and our bodies pressed together, I'd been reduced to nothing more than a lovesick fool. The truth of the matter was, I didn't really mind it. Here, with him, there was nothing but the two of us. "Did you find it?" He nodded and slipped his fingers into my hair, but then I heard a faint *swoosh*. "Everyone, get down!" I shouted as I tackled Alarick to the ground beneath me.

The Cù-Sìth hound let out a terrifying howl that shook the trees. "Foul beasts dare to invade my lands?"

I lifted my head, sending a pulse of magic out so I could see, and I heard Grimm's pained howl.

"Owin!"

Scrambling to my feet, I joined Grimm as he held his mate, who struggled for breath, amber eyes wide with fear. A dead snake beast lay in the grass near them, its throat sliced open.

"What happened?"

"I don't know. One minute he stood next to me, the next he'd shifted and jumped away. That *thing* fell in a bloodied heap, but not before it took a swing at Owin with that arrow, grazing his arm. Then Owin fell suddenly." Grimm motioned over to an arrow plunged into the ground near Owin. I plucked it out of the dirt, the stench burning my nostrils. My blood turned to ice as dread filled me.

"The tip has been coated in venom."

"What?" Alarick asked, kneeling beside us.

"I can't believe he killed that thing on his own. Will he be all right?" Grimm's voice broke as he ran a hand over Owin's head. "Owin, love, please hold on."

"I can heal him, but we need to—"

My words were cut off as the Cù-sìth bellowed, "Incoming!"

Alarick jumped to his feet and threw his hands up to the sky, a pulse of magic protecting us from the dozens upon dozens of venomous arrows soaring toward us.

"This is Nathair's doing," I told Alarick. "He knows regular weapons can't harm you, so he's armed them with something that can."

Before Alarick could ask the questions I saw in his eyes, he flinched.

"What's wrong?"

"The arrows burn against my magic." He lifted his gaze to the shield, and his eyes widened. "They're piercing my shield."

I cursed under my breath. "We need to leave here."

Grimm placed Owin in my arms, and I held him to me, expecting Grimm to open a portal so we could make our escape. Instead he shifted, releasing a howl that shook the leaves of the trees around us. He grew to a monstrous size, fangs bared, silver fur bristling and eyes glowing blue. He'd called upon the powers of his pack.

"Grimm, wait!" Damnation, now was not the time.

Grimm charged the humanoid snakes, some armed with swords, others with bows and arrows. He showed no mercy, sparing none of the foul creatures who'd dared harm his mate. His giant sharp fangs ripped through flesh; his fur became matted with blood. With a haunting howl, the Cù-Sìth alpha joined the fight, green vines shooting from his fur and impaling the beasts.

"I won't be able to hold them back much longer," Alarick said through his teeth, and I gazed up at the sky, the venomous arrows nearly through the shield. The wind howled, the sky darkening as a storm rolled quickly in, Alarick's eyes glowing, his body surrounded by crackling energy and pulsing magic. He gritted his teeth as he attempted to push the arrows out. If even one of those arrows hit Alarick, all would be lost. As it was, Owin gasped for breath, and the arrow had merely scratched the surface of his skin.

"Grimmwolf, your mate needs you!" I called out.

"Go!" the Cù-sìth growled. "I'll hold them off."

"What about you?" I asked.

"My kind and I are connected to the underworld. These beasts cannot harm me. Go!"

Grimm turned and sped toward us while Alarick snapped his fingers and opened a portal. Knowing it would take Grimm some time to shift back to his human form after calling on the power of his pack, I carried Owin and hurried to the portal, sensing Grimm at my heels.

"Alarick, now!" I stopped using my magic and stepped through the portal just as I felt Alarick dash through. It closed behind us, and I sent out a tiny pulse of magic in time to see an arrow had managed to whiz through at the last moment. It struck a vase to Alarick's left, which exploded into hundreds of tiny shards, the flowers shooting out in all directions. "Are you all right?" I asked him.

"Yes," he replied, sounding breathless. "I've never felt such resistance against my power. I feared sending out a blast, with Owin in such a weakened state."

At the mention of his name, Owin groaned, and Grimm howled.

"We need to get him comfortable," I told Grimm, who took off down the corridor. I ran after him, mindful not to jostle Owin too much. His breathing had become labored, his fair skin shockingly pale. I entered their bedchamber and laid Owin carefully on the large bed.

"What do you need?" Alarick asked, taking position at my side.

"We need to remove his shirt, and as Grimm is lacking in opposable thumbs right now, I need you to help me."

Alarick didn't hesitate. He snapped his fingers, making Owin's vest and shirt disappear. A low growl came from Grimm at the sight of the green-and-black veins spreading up Owin's arm from the wound. Grimm howled before he started pacing again, hackles up and teeth bared.

The young ocelot prince groaned.

"Easy," I soothed, petting Owin's soft hair and hoping Grimm calmed as well. "Alarick, I need you to keep Grimm away from Owin. He's not going to like this."

Alarick shifted into his huge white lion form and leapt effortlessly onto the bed, where he positioned himself between Owin and Grimm. Closing my eyes, I put a hand to Owin's brow.

"This is going to hurt, but I promise you will feel better once I'm done."

Owin nodded, and I placed my hands on his arm,

covering the wound. Reaching deep inside myself, I called upon my powers, knowing the moment I was finished, Alarick and I would have to leave. Concentrating on the wound and the evil seeping into Owin's blood, I allowed the connection to be made so the venom recognized the source of one of its own. I gritted my teeth and began to draw the venom out of his body and into my own.

The scream Owin released sent a shiver through me, but I couldn't stop. Not now. His small body arched up off the bed, and Grimm snarled as he lunged toward me, his animal instincts taking control and needing to defend his mate. He didn't get far. Alarick swatted at Grimm with a huge paw, the force of it knocking Grimm onto his side. Alarick hadn't used his claws, but there had been no need to. Grimm was the size of a normal alpha wolf now, his body having redistributed the powers he'd borrowed from his pack. He shifted into his human form, then took a step forward but came to a halt when Alarick hissed.

"Please," Grimm whimpered. "I need to be with him."

"It's all right," I told Alarick. "I'm almost finished. Let him be with his mate."

Alarick jumped off the bed and sat on his haunches beside me as Grimm scrambled onto the mattress.

"What are you doing?" Grimm asked softly, running his fingers through Owin's hair.

"Pulling the venom out of him and into myself."

"Won't that kill you?"

I shook my head, aware of Alarick's intense gaze on me. "No. It will hurt me, but unlike anyone else touched by this poison, I'll be able to heal."

Owin whimpered, and Grimm murmured quiet soothing words to him as I withdrew the last of it. My knees weakened, and I faltered, but Alarick caught me, holding me up.

"Jean, are you all right?"

I nodded. "Just weakened. I'll be fine in a moment."

"Is he going to be okay?" Grimm asked, cradling Owin in his arms.

"Yes. I've stopped the venom from spreading, and his shifter body is healing itself."

"Owin, love?"

"I'm all right," Owin promised weakly. "I'm sorry."

"You have nothing to be sorry for," Grimm replied, rocking him gently. "I love you so much. You're so very brave."

"And fierce," Owin added with a small nod. "I was very fierce."

"Oh, so fierce," Grimm agreed, kissing the top of his head. He lifted his face, tears in his eyes. "Thank you, Lord Eldrich."

"Don't thank me. I put your mate in danger."

"We," Alarick corrected. "We placed you both in danger."

Feeling capable of standing on my own two feet, I gently pushed away from Alarick.

"You needed us," Owin said, his words laced with sleep. "That's what family does."

With a warm smile, Alarick leaned in and ran a hand over Owin's head. "Rest now." He moved his gaze to Grimm. "You as well. Thank you for your help."

Grimm nodded. "Wait, where's the scythe?"

Alarick opened one side of his suit jacket and pulled out a small black-and-silver object.

"Is that... a fountain pen?" Grimm asked, confused.

"It would seem this was the last weapon wielded by a

human." He placed it back in his pocket. "Rest. If you need anything, let us know." With a frown, Alarick turned to me. "I've never seen anything like that. How is it you could do that?"

"We need to leave," I replied.

"Jean—"

"I used my magic to save Owin, which means Nathair is most likely tracking me as we speak. We need to leave. Now."

"Very well." Alarick snapped his fingers and a portal opened.

I hated leaving Grimm and Owin, but the farther we were from them, the safer they would be. Now we had the scythe, we needed a plan. I stopped the use of my magic and stepped through the portal, Alarick close behind.

Were we in a cave? I turned to ask Alarick, but he loomed over me, his eyes narrowed.

"It's time you give me some answers, Jean."

CHAPTER FIVE

ALARICK

"What you did back there shouldn't have been possible," I said, watching Jean pace several feet ahead.

This discussion was long overdue, so I'd brought us somewhere we could talk. The magical cave lay hundreds of feet below the surface, the rock walls lit by thousands of tiny glowworms. I'd visited once in my youth when the responsibilities of my crown seemed overwhelming. The cavernous space gave off a sense of peace, as if no one and nothing existed outside of it.

When Nathair first appeared and Jean was hurt, I hadn't questioned why Jean had been able to heal himself—despite knowing I wouldn't have been so lucky. Nathair had the power to kill me, as did Jean. Nathair planned to assassinate me. Jean was my dearest friend and perhaps... I shook that thought from my head. Now was not the time.

Anger and frustration bubbled to the surface. "How is it

possible I know as much about what Nathair is as I do you?"

Jean whirled around and tore the bandage from around his eyes. "You want to know what I am? Then you will meet the monster inside!"

"Jean—"

Jean threw his arms out, his face turned to the heavens before he burst into green fire. I gasped and took several steps back as shimmering black scales emerged from the flames. They were large and armored, and at first I thought dragon, but no, this was... far more terrifying. The tip of Jean's tail reminded me of a lion, the tufted fur at the tip green. That same fur traveled up his tail, and I tried to peer inside the green flames when Jean sprang forward, his exceptionally long body coiled. He almost looked as if he were made of three creatures—a dragon, serpent, and lion.

"King of the Serpents," I whispered. That was only a formality. A description of how his kind had been referred to in myths and legends. Jean was not a king, but he *was*... a prince.

A basilisk prince.

So many magical creatures had become myths, but I had seen them all in my time on this Earth. Except for basilisks. They were true creatures of legend. Mostly because anyone unfortunate enough to cross paths with a basilisk would never live to tell the tale.

A hiss drew my attention up to Jean's massive head, a combination of serpent and lion, with fangs bigger than me. Green fur surrounded the spikes and scales behind his head, almost like a lion's mane. The same fur lined his jaw. Flat scales extended from the top of his head, standing tall in the shape of a crown. He was the most terrifying creature I had ever laid eyes on, and the most beautiful.

Laid eyes on.

My heart splintered, the cracks tearing wide before my heart broke. Tears filled my eyes as he lowered his head before me. I placed my hand on his brow beside his eye. "Tell me you didn't."

Jean closed his eyes and turned his head away from me.

"No, you look at me," I commanded.

Jean slowly opened his eyes, pools of foggy aquamarine staring back at me from eyes that should have killed me.

A tear rolled down my cheek, and breathing became difficult. "You... you did this to yourself, didn't you? You took your sight. Blinded yourself so you wouldn't hurt me."

Jean released a huff and slowly slithered closer, winding and curling his body around me. More tears threatened to spill, and I fought for control.

"Shift. Please."

A heartbreaking wail escaped him before he lifted himself high, stretching his long body out as he roared and spewed green fire, his large tail thrashing and sending up clouds of dust and smoke.

"Come now. Is that necessary? It's not like you to throw such a tantrum."

Jean came up short, arching his neck and tilting his head to one side as he observed me.

I smiled up at him and placed my hand on one of his scales. "If you believe I think any less of you now that I've seen you, then perhaps you don't know me as well as you think you do."

Jean puffed little bursts of fire and smoke through his nostrils before he laid his enormous head on the ground beside me. I ran my fingers through the fur of his jawline, surprised by how soft it was. I doubted anyone had ever been this close to a basilisk before. If their stare didn't kill you, the venom that dripped from their fangs or the paralyzing fire they spewed certainly would. As a creature older than time itself, it was not one of my shifter children, despite the ability to shift into human form. It was also one of the few creatures that could kill me. A single drop of basilisk venom was enough to cause an agonizing death, even for me.

There was no danger of venom touching me around Jean because he had none. A basilisk's ability to produce venom was connected to its sight, as was the paralyzing agent found in its fire. Jean had rid himself of his greatest power. He groaned, and what was left of my heart broke.

"Please," I begged softly.

Jean shifted, standing before me a rumpled mess, hair in disarray, cheek smudged with dirt, a stark reminder of what he'd done.

I fisted his shirt in my hands. "Never again will you hurt yourself for me. Do you understand?" I'd never felt the urge to throttle him like I did now. "Jean," I pleaded.

He laid his hands over mine, his voice soft. "I cannot promise you that, my king."

"Jean..." I shook my head. "You told me it was a Hantu Buta that blinded you." That night had been forever seared into my mind. Jean had gone off on his own after our return from Athens. I didn't question him. I rarely ever did. Then one night, I heard a chilling moan and found Jean sprawled in the garden, a bloodied bandage over his eyes. Once I'd helped him get cleaned up and into bed, I questioned him. An evil spirit disguised as an old man had feigned distress, and when Jean hurried over to help, the old man blinded him.

"Why? Why would you do such a thing?" I could no longer stop the tears from escaping, and he smiled softly at me, brushing my cheek with his thumb.

"You are as oblivious as you are magnificent, Alarick. I *love* you. I have loved you from the moment you asked me to dance, and not as a friend. I'm *in* love with you. I hadn't even known I had a heart until you made it beat."

My gasp was lost when his lips touched mine, igniting a different manner of fire. An inferno of desire swept through me, setting alight every inch of me. I realized I'd stilled, and Jean must have taken my reaction to mean his advances were unwelcome. How very wrong he was. Before he could move away, I threw my arms around him and brought him hard against me, my mouth on his. The way he melted in my embrace sent a shiver through me. I kissed him until my knees threatened to weaken. His eyes were wide, full lips swollen, and cheeks flushed.

"Alarick?"

"Goddess above."

"Are you all right?" He cupped my face, and I turned my head to kiss his palm. "Talk to me."

"I tried to imagine what it would be like to kiss you."

"And?"

"My imagination pales in comparison to the reality. It's like a galaxy of stars colliding within me. I need to feel you, Jean."

He sucked in a sharp breath. "Are you certain?" Concern etched his features, and a fierce sense of protectiveness the likes of which I'd never felt washed over me. In that instant, I knew I would move the heavens and rock the very foundations of hell for Jean.

I brought him into my arms, our hard bodies pressed together. The flush that colored his cheeks did wicked things to my groin.

"You're everything I never knew I wanted." Our mouths became one, tongues dueling and exploring. I flicked my wrist, opening a portal, then pulled him through it, barely able to contain my smile. "Use your magic. I want you to see this." I closed the portal.

"But... Nathair..."

"Can't find us. Not in here."

His brows drew together in question, so I kissed him, smiling against his lips as the worry melted away.

"Trust me."

"Always," he replied. His magic pulsed, and I took a step back, watching the many expressions cross his face as he took in the scenery around him. At first he appeared confused, then delighted, and finally astonished. He turned to face me, and were he able to cry, I knew he would be shedding tears. "How is this possible?"

I took his hand in mine as I led him up the stairs of the Parthenon, everything around us exactly as it had been on that day. The sun shone bright in a cloudless blue sky, a warm breeze rustling the leaves of the olive tree branches. "You changed my life that day. I wonder if my heart had known then what it does now."

"What's that?" he asked, turning to me, his smile radiant.

"That it had found its other half."

"Alarick, this is... I still can't believe it."

"What good is having the power of the cosmos if you can't use it to build something for the one you love?"

Jean froze, his eyes wide as he stared at me. "You built this... for *me*?"

I nodded.

"But, Alarick, interfering with time is forbidden."

"True. Bringing back the Parthenon as it was the day we danced was out of the question, but I'm connected to the gods, even if I am not one myself. And like any godlike creature, I found a loophole. A pocket outside of time." I winked at him and waited for my previous words to sink in.

A gasp escaped him, and I chuckled. So fierce, yet adorable.

"The one you love. Are you saying that you...?" He seemed to quickly get ahold of himself and rolled his shoulders back before crossing his arms over his chest. "After all these years, I expect a formal declaration."

Yep. Adorable. With a nod, I led him into the temple and stopped before the reflecting pool surrounded by flower petals and gold offerings. Taking both his hands in mine, I kissed his fingers. I wanted to say so much to him, but in the end, I stuck with a few simple words.

"I love you, Jean."

Jean lunged at me, and I laughed against his lips before his tongue found mine. Fire blazed in the wall sconces, tossing shadows across the temple. "A fitting location," I murmured against his lips. "As I plan to worship every inch of you."

All at once we were tearing at each other's clothes until we were both blissfully naked. I took his hand in mine and led him into the warm water of the pool. He pushed me to sit on the wide marble bench to one side and straddled my lap, our hard erections rubbing against each other.

"Goddess above," I breathed, sliding my hands over his back before bringing one to his neck and the other to his plump backside.

"Alarick," Jean pleaded, thrusting his hips, the feel of him intoxicating. He trailed kisses along my jaw, then nipped at my chin, waking a primal hunger inside me I'd never felt before. Claws pierced my fingers, and my eyesight sharpened.

"No one will ever lay a hand on you. You're mine," I

growled, then cringed. "Forgive me. I'm finding it rather difficult to rein myself in. I promised I wouldn't make assumptions. Jean, would you consider being my mate?"

Jean threw his head back and laughed. Not the response I'd expected.

"What?"

"Do you know how long I've wished to hear those words?"

My smile was wide as I nuzzled his temple. "How long?"

"For as long as I've known you." Jean kissed me, and everything around us seemed to slow. He pulled back enough to whisper in my ear. "Unleash your inner beast and claim your mate, my king."

With a roar I stood with him in my arms and carried him outside the clear pool to the thick layer of bedding I'd arranged. I laid him down and turned him onto his stomach. Grabbing one of the many pillows scattered around us, I placed it under his hips and covered his body with mine. He turned his head, and I ravished his lips, my claws plunging into the silky fabric to the sides of his head. With a moan, he lifted his hips, thrusting his beautiful plump asscheeks against me.

"Alarick, please," Jean said through a gasp for breath. "I need you to claim me."

"I should take things slow," I murmured, rubbing my thick hard shaft between his asscheeks. It would be difficult, with every inch of me fighting to claim him, but for Jean, I would do anything.

"There will be time for slow later. Right now, I need you to make me yours. Please, let me be one with you."

"Yes," I growled. What Jean wanted, what I needed at this very moment was beyond coupling. My taking a mate changed the very world around us. If something should happen to me, I took comfort knowing my shifter children would have a new father, for everything I was would become his as well once I joined us as one. Jean knew what being my mate entailed. He'd been with me long enough to know everything about me.

"Are you sure you want a basilisk for a mate?"

I took hold of his chin and kissed him hard. "I want *you* as my mate, Jean. What you are is of little consequence to me, but in case you need to hear the words, I believe you to be the most beautiful creature I have ever seen."

"Then I am yours," Jean said on a happy sigh.

I snapped my fingers, lube appearing in my hand. "Being king has its perks." Jean laughed as I wriggled my eyebrows. I kissed him again, needing to taste him more than I needed air in my lungs. I pressed a finger to his entrance, and his moan had me sucking in a sharp breath. "Forgive me," I said, breathless, as I placed a kiss to his shoulder, my finger entering his beautiful body.

"For what?" Jean asked, skin flushed. His soft moan sent a pulse of need flaring through me. I added a second finger, and he trembled beneath me.

"For not realizing sooner that we were meant for each other." I nipped at his ear and whispered, "Are you ready for me?"

"Yes, Alarick! Dear Goddess, yes!"

I grinned and lined my shaft up with his pink hole, mindful as I pressed the tip against his entrance. Jean hissed, and I paused, fearful I'd hurt him, but Jean was having none of my tenderness. He impaled himself back, and our shouts echoed through the cavernous temple. I cursed loudly and attempted to gather myself.

"Jean—"

"You've never seen me as fragile," Jean growled. "Don't you dare start now."

Something inside me burst free. I took hold of his hips and pulled out before slamming back into him, burying myself deep inside him. He let out a strangled cry and threw an arm back, his nails digging into my flesh.

"Don't you dare stop."

It was a little terrifying how fiercely I needed him, and I refused to think about the depths I would go to for him. He was my mate. Or at least he would be momentarily. For so long he'd been at my side, protecting me, caring for me, cherishing me, and that's what I was: cherished. I might not have realized it then, but somewhere deep inside I'd known it. It was the reason I'd wanted him at my side from the instant we met. I thrust my hips forward, my muscles tense as I plunged myself deep inside him over and over. Sweat glistened his back, and I ran a hand up his spine to his shoulder, taking hold of it, then his hip with the other and pounded into him like a wild beast.

I gave Jean what we both wanted, our bodies joined in a dance of unbridled need and explosive passion. My muscles tightened, the wind whipping through the temple as my powers swirled around us, the flames from the wall sconces bursting higher as I made Jean mine. His body was beautiful—long, sleek, toned. Pale, flawless skin, strong arms and legs, a tapered waist. No one was smarter, more patient and kind. And he was mine.

My eyesight sharpened, lightning crackling around us as my hips sped up. Thunder rumbled through the temple, and I lay over Jean's back as I drove in deep again and again, our panting breaths mingling.

"Alarick!" Jean's body stilled as he spilled himself, and it was more than I could stand. My orgasm burst through me, and I sank my elongated fangs into the flesh of Jean's shoulder. Jean's shout echoed around us, and I snapped my hips again, my body on fire as I spilled myself inside him. Power surged through me and into Jean. I retracted my fangs, and my shout combined with Jean's as my magic burst out of us, exploding into millions of tiny stars, the illusion of the temple around us flickering as it struggled to stay intact, infiltrated by the silent beauty of the cosmos.

I'd emptied myself when Jean let out a snarling hiss. He moved faster than light, and I found myself on my back, Jean straddling me. His eyes had gone from their usual aquamarine to pitch-black, the faintest hint of scales beneath his skin.

"Tell me not to," he demanded.

I brushed my fingers down his cheek. "I won't do that."

"Alarick..."

"I am not ashamed of what you are."

"What if I hurt you?"

"I will survive."

"How do you know?"

"Because we are one. Because I love you."

Jean brought our lips together in a fiery kiss before he tore himself away and sank his fangs into my neck. I gasped, my back arching up off the floor. Jean might no longer have any venom, but the fire inside him burned through me, making me feel as if I were going to ignite from the inside out. The pain was excruciating, but I gritted my teeth, the tears slipping free at the corners of my eyes. Green fire burst from my eyes and my body convulsed, the fire soon replaced by a cool, soothing balm.

"Alarick?" Jean wiped my tears.

"I'm fine, love."

Jean lay on me, his head on my shoulder. I wrapped my

arms around him and ran a soothing hand over his hair. Holding him to me felt right, as if I'd been doing it my whole life. Thinking back, I could kick myself. I'd spent so long finding mates for my shifter children, I never considered finding one for myself. I couldn't imagine anyone out there being a good fit, not realizing the one meant for me had been at my side the entire time.

"I hadn't intended on claiming you," he murmured. "Why did you allow it?"

"For the same reason you asked me to claim you." I'd wanted to be as much a part of Jean as he wished to be a part of me.

Jean released a happy sigh, and my heart swelled. He fit so perfectly against me. I rolled us over so I could see him better. He lay facing me, a shy smile on his flushed face. It was the sweetest thing I'd ever seen. When it came to defending me, no one was fiercer than Jean. He had little tolerance for injustice and wouldn't hesitate to rid the world of evil. Yet with me, he was tender, gentle, so caring. He brushed my hair away from my eyes.

"I love you, Alarick."

"I love you too, Jean." I kissed him, and he released another happy sigh. For the first time in my existence, I was uncertain about the future. Fear was a new concept for me, and although I didn't fear death at the hands, or rather fangs, of Nathair, I feared losing Jean. "What would I do without you?"

"You would be sad," he whispered as he absently stroked the fine hairs on my chest. He'd said those words to me not long ago, and they squeezed at my heart now just as much as they had then.

"I would be lost," I murmured, bringing him in close to

me and shutting my eyes when he began to pepper kisses across my shoulder and chest.

"You must not say such things."

"I speak only the truth." I ran my fingers through his hair, our legs intertwined.

He pulled back, his smile radiant and lighting up his handsome face before he seemed to recall something. "Alarick, have you considered what sort of effect our mating will have on us?"

Jean's question reminded me of at least one reason I'd never taken a mate. There was no telling what my claiming them would do to them. My mate would have to be powerful in their own right in order to survive my power flowing through them. I never doubted Jean's power, but having seen his true form confirmed he was even stronger than I'd originally believed. I never would have accepted him as my mate if I'd had even the tiniest doubts. I'd never do anything to hurt Jean.

"I knew you'd be able to survive my power flowing through you," I said as I watched the galaxies swirling around us, the infinite expanse of space visible through the illusions I'd created of the Parthenon. "But I admit, I have no idea how my power mixing with yours will affect you and vice versa. Only time will tell."

"I suppose we should devise a plan to stop Nathair." He kissed my chin as he caressed my chest. "I wish we could stay here, just like this."

"Me too. But if we're to start out new future together, we must rid ourselves of this assassin." I lifted his chin and pressed a kiss to his soft lips. "I've found my mate. I won't let anyone take you away from me."

It was time to get rid of Nathair once and for all.

CHAPTER SIX

JEAN

I DIDN'T FEEL any different. At least not inside.

Being mated to Alarick was something I'd never dreamed could happen, so the effects of such a mating was something I'd not considered until this point. I supposed only time would tell, though I doubted I'd have that much time. I couldn't allow myself to get excited about our future together, because the likelihood I would survive this was slim.

I watched Alarick dress, and my heart felt heavy despite this being the happiest day of my life. After all this time, he was finally mine, and I'd likely not get to enjoy him. Knowing this might be the last time I saw him, I pulsed my magic, using as much of it as possible to sear his image into my mind. It wasn't as if I hadn't mapped out every inch of him over the millenniums, but I saw him through different eyes now. He was so beautiful, a white light in the darkness, brighter than any star in the heavens, warm and good, always here to guide me.

"I suppose it will change when we're closer to Nathair."

I snapped my head up. "Pardon?"

"The scythe," he replied with a frown, holding up the god-killing weapon still in the form of a fountain pen.

"I hope so." I stood in front of him, fully dressed, the soreness in my backside a wonderful reminder of the amazing sex.

"You're blushing," he said with a chuckle. He brought me close against him, murmuring in my ear. "I can't stop thinking about it either. Your gorgeous body, naked, under me as I drive into your tight heat over and over."

"You're incorrigible. Here we are about to go into battle and you're teasing me." I adjusted myself, growling at his soft laugh.

"As soon as this is over, I plan to take you home to *our* bed and have my way with you time and time again. Perhaps you might like to have your way with me as well."

I gaped at him. "You want that?"

His smile had me melting against him. "Jean, when it comes to you, I want it all." He kissed me breathless, his mouth making a meal out of mine. I wrapped my arms around his neck as he squeezed me to him, hands roaming my back, then sliding down to squeeze my backside. He ground his hips against mine, and I released a moan. I'd not wanted anyone or anything so desperately in all of my life. With a sigh, he pulled away and rested his brow against mine.

"We *will* get through this. I need to wake up every morning to your beautiful face." He cupped my cheek. "And go to sleep at night with you in my arms after making love to you. I need a thousand more lifetimes with you, Jean."

Unable to get any words past the lump in my throat, I nodded. He released me, and I managed to suppress a whimper at the loss.

"All right, let's think this through. We have the weapon." He paced the marble floor in front of the reflecting pool, the fire of the wall sconces casting dancing shadows across his figure.

"I should be the one to kill him," I blurted.

He stopped and turned to me with a frown. "Jean, I'm the one he wishes to kill. Nathair will go through you to get to me."

"I may go down, but I will take that bastard with me!"

"No!" Alarick's bellow shook the very foundations of the palace around us. I stared at him, dumbstruck. I'd never seen him so furious. He marched over to me and took hold of my arms, his expression softening. "I won't allow you to sacrifice yourself for me. We will defeat Nathair together, and we will return home *together*."

"Alarick—"

"No," Alarick replied through his teeth. "I will not budge on this, Jean. So help me, I will banish you to another realm and go after Nathair myself if for a moment I believe you're going to forfeit your life to that monster."

My sigh was heavy. "So damned stubborn."

He smiled beautifully before pressing a kiss to my lips. "Yes, I am. Now, we need a plan." He walked away from me, chuckling at my cursing under my breath. "Once you shift, Nathair will appear."

"Correct."

"What we need is to distract him so he doesn't see me coming."

"Speaking of seeing, the moment you catch his eye, he'll hypnotize you, and then you're as good as dead, Alarick."

"There is that," Alarick muttered. "I'll have to blindfold myself."

I arched an eyebrow at him. "And then what?"

Alarick's smile was sheepish. "I was hoping you could give me a few tips?"

We were doomed. "Alarick, I have spent thousands of years honing my senses and my magic to see for me. It's not something you can simply do because you wish it. You have to rely completely on your other senses. Anticipate and act rather than react."

"I have to try, Jean."

His soft-spoken words cut me to the quick. With a heavy sigh, I reached into my pocket and removed the silk bandage. "Come here." As soon as he stood before me, I wrapped the bandage around his eyes, securing it firmly at the back of his head. "Close your eyes."

"Okay."

I took his hand in mine and led him outside. "Can Nathair portal himself here?"

"No. This place doesn't exist on any plane. As I created it, only I can transport someone here." Alarick followed as I led him down the stairs of the Parthenon he'd created for us and to an expansive garden filled with olive trees, fragrant flowers, and stone pathways. "Listen to the world around you. What do you hear?"

"Water trickling from a nearby fountain, the leaves rustling in the breeze, and birds chirping."

I took several steps away from him, then shifted, his form growing smaller as I stretched my serpent's body up.

"Jean?"

Silently I slithered around him. He sniffed the air.

"You've shifted."

I coiled around him and nudged him with my head, making him laugh. He petted my fur mane before I pulled away. My body didn't make a sound. He tilted his head, listening for me, but I knew he wouldn't hear me. Not unless I purposefully made noise. I needed Alarick to understand what he would be facing. Summoning courage, I lashed out at him with my tail, and he went flying, smacking into a tree. He dropped to the ground with a groan.

I hissed at him, and he held his hands up in front of him. "Okay, I understand. Attack me again." He snapped his fingers, a long bo stick appearing in his hand in place of whatever weapon he'd be using against Nathair. I slithered away from him, my mind telling me this was pointless. How could Alarick defeat something he could neither see nor hear? But my heart scolded me, telling me to have faith in my beloved.

"What's the matter, Jean? Getting slow in your old age?"

Old age? *Old age!* I hissed and whipped my tail at him again, stunned when he leapt over it and smacked it with the stick. He laughed in triumph, at least until I swept his feet out from under him. He crashed onto his backside with a curse. I blew out a puff of smoke as I tilted my head happily.

He laughed. "Proud of yourself, are you?"

I huffed out smoke through my nostrils in response. Slithering away again, I studied him, watching as he tilted his head, listening for any sound. I lifted the end of my tail to strike, but Alarick spoke up.

"Goodness, Jean, at this rate Nathair will expire from old age."

With a growl I thrust my tail in his direction, only for him to jump over it again and smack me with the stick. Annoyed, I hissed and roared, moving around him and whipped my tail at him. Again he jumped and whacked me.

"I quite enjoy this game."

Game? I'd show him game. I blew out fire at his insolence and slithered swiftly around him, ready to gather him up in my long body and squeeze, but he continued to jump out of my reach. I roared, green flames spewing from my mouth as I lunged for him, getting smacked in the snout. Shrieking, I slithered away, but then I realized what he was doing. Oh! Such a sneaky bastard. I lowered myself to the ground and stilled. He grinned wide.

"Caught on, did you?"

I huffed.

"It's a long shot, I know, but if I can provoke Nathair, then I have a chance. I simply have to hear him coming."

"And if you don't?" I asked after shifting back into human form. "If he's not easily provoked?"

Alarick's grin was smug. "Come now, Jean. I'm an expert at finding the perfect way to frustrate even the most steadfast." He motioned toward me, and I shook my head, doing my best not to smile. He wasn't wrong.

"Very well, but if I caught on to your game, it's only a matter of time before he will catch on as well."

"Then I should probably kill him before then, huh?"

"Oh, well, in that case, why worry?" My words dripped with sarcasm, and I folded my arms over my chest.

"Aw, come now, Jean." Alarick brought me into his arms and kissed me. I shamefully submitted without question, taking everything he was willing to give me. I chased his lips when he pulled away, and he smiled. "How about some more practice, then?"

"Alarick—"

"Please." He kissed the tip of my nose. "Humor me."

"Very well." We each walked to the farthest ends of the garden away from each other. I shifted, my giant mass spreading, black scales shimmering in the sunlight. I coiled my body and lowered my head as Alarick readied himself, bo stick in hand. This time I remained silent, and Alarick made no attempt to aggravate me. He simply stood and listened.

Slowly I slithered around the garden, and Alarick stiffened. He sniffed the air. I waited for him to speak about whatever he'd sensed, but he simply resumed his position and waited for me. A small smile tugged at his lips. What did he know that I didn't?

Readying myself, I moved in, silent, arching up and lifting my tail. Changing my mind, I lowered my tail. If Alarick wanted to do this, then I wouldn't go easy on him. I struck out at him, my fangs bared. He leapt to one side, smacking me on the side of the head with his stick. I roared at him, more surprised he'd managed to strike me than anything. How was that possible?

Speeding away, I coiled in on myself, then sprang at him. Again, he jumped and struck me on the head. Arching my neck, I rose to my full height. How was he doing this? I spewed green fire at him, and he rolled out of the way seconds before the flames could touch him. I retreated and attacked several times, each one ending with me getting batted on the head. It didn't hurt. My scales were impenetrable. Only the fangs of another basilisk could get through my defenses, and even so it wouldn't be easy.

Time and time again, I struck at him and was met with defeat. I finally shifted back into my human form. "How are you doing that?"

"It's the most amazing thing, Jean." Alarick removed the blindfold from around his eyes and shoved it into his pocket. "Suddenly I could sense your heat. I could feel the vibration of your body on the ground as you moved. Your scent, your heat, the vibration, all of it came together to form a clear picture in my mind, as if I could *see* you."

I stared at him. "That's impossible. Only a basilisk—" My eyes widened, and his expression softened.

"You gave me this gift, Jean."

Alarick pulled me into his arms, and I laid my head on his chest, my heart threatening to beat out of me. Some of my power had transferred to him. I didn't know how much of it or to what extent, but for the first time, I felt as if we might be able to pull this off. I lifted my face and kissed his jaw.

"Despite these gifts, remember I have no venom. You must stay away from his fangs and whatever venom he spits at you. We can't leave something like that to chance. If even the tip of one of his fangs grazes you..."

"Yes, I know, love." Alarick kissed me, and I surrendered myself to the moment, enjoying the feel of his lips on mine, the taste of his tongue, and heat of his mouth. I inhaled his scent, relished the feel of his body against me as the birds chirped and the sun shone down on us. Whatever happened, this right here was perfect, and I would never forget it. We kissed as if it were our last day on Earth, and I supposed it could be. "Have faith," Alarick whispered in my ear before kissing my cheek. He took hold of my hand. "Where should we go?"

"Somewhere remote. Big enough for a battle but away from civilization. It needs to offer cover." It didn't matter that Nathair would also find places to hide. We needed the cover to be able to escape or regroup if needed. Alarick snapped his fingers and opened a portal. I looked back at the Parthenon, a wistful sigh escaping me.

"Don't worry. We'll return soon."

I kissed Alarick's cheek and stopped all use of my magic as we stepped through the portal, just in case. Once the portal closed, I sent out a small pulse of magic to see where Alarick had taken us. I'd heard stories of when he'd visited this place for the birth of his first elk. He'd been so proud. We appeared in a lush green forest, and although on first glance it could be any forest, this one was untouched by humans. A thick fog blanketed the ground, light struggling to claw its way through the dense treetops. Come nightfall, the forest would be pitch-black.

We trekked into the woods, nothing but an ocean of trees stretching before us.

"What about his followers?" I asked Alarick. They would be along soon, and my guess was they would be armed with more venom-tipped weapons.

"Followers?"

Surely he hadn't thought Nathair would simply show up and face us on his own. "Alarick, Nathair won't be alone."

"Neither will you."

We turned, a gasp escaping both of us as portal after portal opened and Alarick's shifter children stepped through. Every shifter prince and princess appeared, along with their mates if they had one. Thousands of them.

I smiled. "My father's fear has come to pass."

"What?"

"He feared you would raise an army of shifters too powerful to defeat."

"But they were not raised to be warriors, Jean."

"You're wrong," Sinopa said as she approached. "We've trained our whole lives for this."

Alarick shook his head, confused. "Trained? I never issued any orders for training."

Grimm stepped forward, his hand in Owin's. "You didn't," he said with a warm smile before moving his gaze to me. "But Lord Eldrich did."

Alarick turned to face me. "Jean? I don't understand."

"The quests," I replied, cupping his cheek. "I might not have known about Nathair, but I knew one day your life would be at risk. No great power goes unchallenged forever, my love. My father's fears gave me much to think about, and then it struck me. I proposed that each of your ruling shifter children be put through a quest to prove their worth. It would test them in ways they had never been tested. Each prince and princess taught their children to be ready for the day their quest would come. They were taught to hone their magic, their skills, to embrace challenge with courage and ferocity. They fought, not for their crown, but for others, for those they loved, as I love you."

Alarick sucked in a sharp breath. "You... did all this? For me?"

I kissed him, laughing against his lips at the thunderous cheers and catcalls from his children. We laid our foreheads together before Alarick turned to face the princes and princesses.

"Are you certain you want to do this? I would never put any of you at risk."

"We know," Owin replied. "You also have a bad habit of making decisions for us, and that ends now, with us here choosing to fight for you."

Bernd stepped forward, his mate, Saer, at his side. "Nathair killed my father. I won't lose you as well."

My heart swelled at Bernd's words, and a lump formed in my throat at the familiar faces. They were all so young. A whole new generation of princes and princesses, all ready to go to war for their king. No, not just their king, but for the father of all, the king who had given birth to their kind.

Tears filled Alarick's eyes. "Thank you. All of you." He turned to face me. "And thank you."

I brought his fingers to my lips for a kiss. "Today we end this."

Determination and resolve filled Alarick's eyes. He kissed me, a quick but passionate kiss on the lips. "Today we end this."

CHAPTER SEVEN

ALARICK

"Ready?" I asked Jean.

He nodded, but I felt how nervous he was. I placed a hand to his cheek and kissed him in front of all my shifter children so everyone could see what he meant to me. Jean's soft lips pulled into a sweet smile.

"They love you, Jean. That won't change once they see."

"Thank you," Jean replied quietly.

I'd sent word out on the wind into the ears of each of the princes, princesses, and their mates that Jean was going to reveal himself so they didn't have to rely on scent alone to tell him apart from Nathair. Although Jean informed us Nathair was smaller than him and his appearance was more of a cross between snake and eel, I didn't want anyone to mistake Jean for an enemy.

Releasing a shaky breath through his mouth, Jean stood

back and shifted, his serpent's body growing and stretching until he rose above them. Gasps were heard en masse, and Jean lowered his head to the ground, his body coiled as if trying to make himself smaller. I put my hand to the side of his head and petted the fur on his jaw.

Owin was the first to take a step forward. He smiled tentatively at Jean before reaching out and placing a delicate hand on Jean's nose. Jean huffed out a small puff of green smoke, ruffling Owin's hair and making him laugh.

After that, my shifter children rushed Jean, all wanting to feel his scales or touch him, their eyes filled with awe. Next to me, they were the only ones to have ever seen a basilisk and live. With Jean's permission, I sent word to each of them, telling them all how they mustn't so much as glance in the direction of Nathair's eyes. Unlike Jean, who had no venom and therefore couldn't kill them, Nathair would paralyze them, then strike with a poisonous blow. They were to stick to fighting off Nathair's followers and protecting themselves.

Jean shifted back and turned to face me. "It's time. Nathair knows I'm here."

I nodded and brought him up against me to kiss him thoroughly. Once he was breathless, we pulled apart. He gave me a flirty smile before heading off. My heart swelled as he disappeared into the woods. Once he was gone, I turned to my shifter children, all of whom were smiling knowingly at me.

"Yes, well, there's that." I smiled warmly at them, my heart overflowing with pride. "I couldn't have asked for more wonderful children. Please be careful out there, and know that I love you all so much." They shifted into their animal forms, from the tiniest hummingbird to the largest whale. I waved my hand, sending my magic pulsing off so my aquatic children could swim through the air as if it were water. I sent another pulse of magic out, wrapping each one in a protective shield. As long as I drew breath, my magic would help protect them.

Whatever happened, I couldn't allow Nathair to win. There was far too much at stake.

I removed my suit jacket and laid it on the log beside me before rolling up my sleeves to my elbows. I still couldn't believe everything that had happened in the last day. My heart danced joyously at the memory of Jean. I had a mate. A beautiful, kind, wonderful mate who knew me better than I knew myself.

Never would I have imagined Jean's affections for me had actually been him in love with me. We'd been together for so long, and his behavior toward me had never changed. He'd always taken good care of me, always been gentle and sweet. How was I supposed to know? My heart ached for him. Having spent so long at my side in love with me and my never knowing. Or perhaps a part of me had known and pretended otherwise? Losing Jean wouldn't have been an option for me, and perhaps somewhere deep inside, my heart feared I would lose Jean had I declared my love and he not reciprocate. Goddess above. And here I thought this sort of thing was for youngsters and not immortals who'd been around since the dawn of time.

Then came the second biggest revelation of my lifetime. Jean had been secretly training my shifter children, preparing them for the day something would come along to threaten our existence.

"I'm happy you found your mate."

I turned wide eyes to Sinopa, sitting serenely on the moss-covered log. Where the blasted hell had she come from? She looked so out of place, all that sharp white against a sea of green.

"You know, huh?"

"Know?" she scoffed. "Your Majesty, we *felt* it when you made the connection."

"You did?"

She nodded. "It was like the world had tilted off its axis, jarring at first, but then set to rights again. Everything was brighter, more colorful. Like the world had been given new life. He's the perfect match for you."

I smiled warmly at the thought of Jean. "He is."

"Took you long enough."

"It would seem everyone knew but me."

Sinopa's eyes twinkled with mischief. "We did. For a very, very, *very* long time."

I grunted in response, making her laugh.

"I still can't believe Lord Eldrich is a basilisk."

"Once Nathair is dead, he will truly be the last of his kind." In a way it saddened me, but then we'd have a world filled with unrivaled assassins. I reminded myself that Jean's kin had been nothing like him. It struck me that even back then, Jean had been one of a kind. A basilisk capable of love.

"It's terrifying," Sinopa said softly, bringing me out of my thoughts.

"I know. But he will never be alone, nor know fear for what he is."

"Are you worried he'll be hunted?"

"They will have to get through me," I growled fiercely.

"Hey, it's okay. We would never let anything happen to him."

"Thank you." It was a small fear in the back of my mind. Once word got out, it was only a matter of time before some foolish hunter of magical creatures attempted to turn Jean into their trophy. They wouldn't get anywhere near him. I'd make sure of it. My shifter children were scattered all over the globe, outnumbering both humans and other magical creatures. If there was so much as a whisper against Jean, I would know of it.

The wind rustled my hair and whispered in my ear. I smiled at Jean's voice.

"It's time. I can feel him."

"Is everyone ready?" I asked, hearing thousands of soft replies confirming they were.

I blew out a breath. "I love you, Jean."

"And I love you, Alarick."

Silence met my ears, and then a terrifying roar echoed in the distance. Jean answered with a roar of his own.

"Nathair is here." I reached into my pocket and pulled out the weapon.

"Is... is that a pen?" Sinopa asked, gaping at the tiny object.

"It's the scythe." Goddess above, it better be, or I was in big trouble. I held it before me. "I am in need of a weapon to defeat my enemy."

The pen glowed blue, slowly wavering as it began to morph, growing thin and long. When it was done, Sinopa let out a bark of laughter.

"That scythe certainly has a morbid sense of humor."

I blinked at the shovel in my hands. "Are you seriously expecting me to kill a giant deadly basilisk with a shovel?" Damn the gods and their twisted imagination.

The scythe once again morphed. This time into a... scythe.

"I feel good about this," Sinopa teased.

The scythe was long, its blade expansive and black with

ancient glowing green glyphs engraved into the metal. I nodded and lifted my gaze to Sinopa. "Be safe."

She hopped off the log and threw her arms around me, hugging me tight. "You and Jean stay alive." With that she shifted, and her small arctic fox form bounded off into the tall grass.

Taking a deep steady breath, I shifted into my giant lion form, but instead of my usual snow-white fur, I changed it to black so I could become one with the shadows. I picked up the scythe with my jaws and took off into the trees. I silently maneuvered from shadow to shadow, my huge paws not making a sound on the soft moss-covered floor of the forest.

In the distance Nathair roared, and I hurried toward him. The only way to kill him would be to remove his head from his body. Battle cries filled the air, hundreds upon hundreds of portals opening. Nathair's putrid followers flooded out. Creatures from the depths of hell I hadn't seen since the dawn of time scurried out, fangs dripping, bodies smelling of rotten flesh. Some had four legs, some six or more, with snake tails and forked tongues. They looked like hounds crossed with snakes.

My shifter children attacked, some in their shifted form, others in their human form with weapons. They worked together as teams, playing off one another's strength. Leaving Nathair's minions to them, I sniffed the air and followed Jean's scent farther into the forest. An explosion of green flames made me still. Jean roared, and I felt his pain down to my bones. I hurried in his direction, mindful not to give away my position, and used the wind to disguise my scent.

More green flames and smoke burst through the trees, and this time it was Nathair's roar that shook the ground beneath my feet. Jean had gotten a good hit in. *That's it, my love. You show that bastard what you're made of.*

Jean's roar once more filled the air as he struck again, Nathair's painful cry resonating. I didn't know if Jean had heard me, but in case he did, I offered up encouragement with my thoughts. *You are a basilisk prince. He should bow down to you.*

The trees shook and the earth quaked as Jean roared, and I lowered myself to the ground. I was close enough to see them now. As we'd discussed, I lay in wait while Jean distracted Nathair. He coiled himself tight, then sprang. Nathair wasn't as big as Jean, but he was equally terrifying with his oily black scales and serpent's head, giant fangs dripping with venom. Spikes protruded from the sides, top, and back of his head, as well as his tail. He was almost as fast as Jean.

The two basilisks twisted their long bodies along each other, stretching tall, nearly hitting the treetops. Their tails thrashed, uprooting trees in their wake. Roars echoed around them, green smoke and flames sporadically bursting around them. Jean coiled around Nathair and squeezed, but Nathair wasn't about to let Jean get the upper hand. He threw himself to the ground, bringing Jean with him, rolling so Jean was beneath him.

My heart pounded fiercely. Now. I had to strike now.

Scythe firmly in my jaws, I stalked around behind Nathair. Gingerly, I grew wings. As King of All Shifters, having the ability to call upon certain traits of whatever animals I chose came in handy. Jean snapped his jaws at Nathair, and I shot up into the air, making a dive for Nathair's neck. Having heard my wings, Nathair made to turn his head, but Jean sank his fangs into his neck. Not hesitating, I readied myself for the strike, but Nathair lashed out with his tail. Knowing I'd be dead if one of those spikes caught my flesh, I was forced into some creative aerial maneuvering.

Damn it, I had to strike Nathair while Jean had his jaws around him and Nathair couldn't catch my eye. I flew up and over, dove, and just scraped by, missing one of the spikes by some of my mane's fluff. Nathair shrieked, and this time when he whipped his tail, it was at Jean and not me. The spikes of Nathair's tail caught Jean on the side of his head, and he reared back with a roar. Before Jean could strike, Nathair struck him again with his tail, the force of it sending Jean tumbling through the forest, ripping up trees and shrubbery as he went.

Goddess above! I prayed Jean wasn't hurt.

I dropped onto the ground and shifted into human form to quickly fish the silk fabric from my pocket and wrap it around my eyes. There was no way I could attack Nathair without it now. I put some distance between us, the scythe gripped tight in my hands. From this point forward, I'd need to rely on my magic and Jean's to see. A throaty chuckle met my ear, and I focused on the sounds around me. I felt the vibration on the ground as Nathair slithered closer, caught his scent in the air.

"If you think you can defeat me, you're more delusional than I thought you were."

Jean appeared behind me. He'd moved faster than I'd been able to hear, but his scent filled my nostrils, and I took comfort in his presence.

"You're both fools," Nathair said with a hiss.

I wondered why Nathair was able to speak in his basilisk form, while Jean didn't. It must have something to do with his eyes. So much of his basilisk powers seemed tied to his sight.

"I'm going to kill you, King Alarick. And then I will rid myself of your prince."

"Not going to happen," I growled, readying myself.

Nathair reeled back and opened his mouth. Before I knew what the hell was happening, I was soaring through the air. I landed roughly, with a groan, just as Jean roared. What the—

The putrid scent of venom filled my nostrils, and I scrambled to my feet with a gasp. "Jean?"

Jean thrashed on the ground in pain, his tail thudding so hard against the earth it splintered my heart. It took me a heartbeat to realize what had happened. Nathair had spit venom at me, and Jean had pushed me out of the way. He must have been hit somewhere vulnerable, most likely a wound he'd received from Nathair. If venom entered one of his open wounds, he'd be in a terrible amount of pain as the venom coursed through his system.

My instinct was to remove the bandage and run to Jean, but the moment I did, I would be dead, and Jean's sacrifice would be for nothing. Nathair slithered toward Jean, and my heart nearly pounded out of me. He meant to strike a final blow and kill Jean.

"Hey!" I shouted. "Do you see this?"

Nathair scoffed. "Your pathetic weapon doesn't scare me."

"It should," I said with a wicked grin. "Because it's the one thing that can kill you."

Nathair huffed out a surprised puff of smoke. "The Scythe of Kronos?"

"That's right. I have the one weapon that can kill you. Come and get it." I turned and sped off into the woods, Nathair's roar echoing through the forest. Furious didn't begin to cover it. I leapt over fallen logs and small streams, making sure not to run into trees. Nathair wasn't even trying to be silent, his huge, thick frame crushing everything in his wake, knocking over trees and splintering logs. Damn it, I needed a new plan.

Venom splattered against a treetop to the right of me, and I cursed under my breath. Wonderful, because being chased by a basilisk wasn't bad enough, now the bastard was flinging venom at me. What the hell was I supposed to do now? Another splatter of venom struck a tree to my left. Well, not get dead was certainly one thing I could do.

"You'll not live through this, shifter king!"

"Thanks for the encouragement." I sprang my feathered wings and took off, flying high into the treetops. Nathair roared, spewing green flames as high as he could. That fool was setting the entire forest ablaze! I needed a plan—or that had been my thought before Nathair skidded to a halt. Instead of chasing me, he headed back in the direction he'd come. In the distance, Nathair's beasts were still at war with my shifter children, though hundreds of the putrid snake-hounds lay motionless on the ground.

Where was Nathair—

"Jean!" I flapped my wings as fast as I could manage, overtaking Nathair to land in front of Jean, who hissed and weakly thrashed his tail. His body was still healing from the venom infecting his wounds and his blood. Jean shoved at me with his nose, but I simply put a hand to it. "Easy, love. There's no way I'm going to let that bastard kill you."

Jean groaned his displeasure, but I wasn't going to leave him. We would get out of this alive together, or not at all. Nathair sped toward me, and I readied the scythe. I lunged at him just as he sprang forward, the scythe swinging fiercely with all my force behind it. It missed his neck, but it ripped out one of his fangs. It flew through the trees and landed somewhere to the left, several feet away.

With an earsplitting shriek, Nathair recoiled, his head thrashing at the pain of losing a deadly weapon. I grinned and readied myself for the strike I knew would be coming. Nathair was livid. If I had to get rid of him piece by piece, then I would do so. I forced myself to still. Battle cries filled the air, and Nathair laughed wickedly.

"Hear that? It's the sound of your children dying."

I shook my head. "I have every faith in them. They *will* destroy every one of your foul beasts, and you know it."

With a hiss, Nathair slithered away. The ground vibrated beneath me as his body moved in a wide circle around us. I made certain to keep myself between him and Jean. The bastard knew the quickest way to me was through Jean. A hiss caught my ear, and Jean moved behind me.

"What are you doing? You need to heal."

Jean struck out at Nathair, and I quickly stepped away. The two coiled around each other and Nathair spit venom at Jean, only this time it landed on the crown on Jean's head, the venom dripping down the tips but doing nothing. I took the opening, spreading my wings and speeding toward Nathair's raised neck. He twisted his head to see me, and Jean plunged his fangs into Nathair's neck, holding him in place. This was it. Jean had him pinned. Pulling back the scythe, I prepared to swing, but Nathair threw his head back, pulling Jean with him. I whirled away just as Jean's head soared past. Agonizing pain shot through my side, and I gasped as every muscle in my body seized.

Nathair thrashed violently, knocking Jean off him and whipping the spikes of his tail into Jean. We both hit the ground, making the earth beneath us quake. The scythe lay at my side as I gasped for breath. Turning my head, I dropped my gaze to my side and the large angry black slash bubbling at my flesh. Jean roared weakly as my body convulsed, paralyzed from the venom working its way through me. How was it possible? I'd stayed away from Nathair's tail.

Nathair's evil laugh echoed around us. "Oh, how ironic. In the end, your venomless lover becomes the source of your downfall."

It was only then I realized Jean's crown had scraped my side when Nathair had jerked him back. Jean's anguished wail broke my heart. I wanted to comfort him but couldn't so much as speak. Nathair loomed over me, the tip of a spike reaching for the bandage around my eyes.

"Let's see those pretty eyes of yours."

CHAPTER EIGHT

JEAN

"Alarick!"

I'd shifted into my human form, needing to be with him. I fought the pain in my body, hated the burning in the back of my eyes, knowing no tears would be forthcoming even though I felt him there. I'd done this. After all this time, all the years of protecting him, I still managed to poison him.

"I'm so sorry," I cried, pushing up onto my hands and knees. "Alarick." My body fought me, but I struggled through the pain just as Nathair tore the bandage off Alarick's face. "No!" My scream took on a grave echo, a storm blasting through the trees as the heavens seemed to shift, the stars pulsing, and a surge of magic the likes of which I'd never felt exploded through me as lightning crashed to the earth, striking Nathair and sending him crashing back into the trees. Fire erupted around him, and he hissed, tail thrashing as he tried to escape.

Had that... had that come from me?

Nathair leapt from the ring of fire and landed near Alarick. "I shall take pleasure in killing the King of All Shifters!"

I felt sick to my stomach as I forced myself onto shaky legs. "Get away from him!" Another burst of magic flared out of me, but Nathair dropped to the ground near Alarick, the magic sweeping over him instead of blasting through him. He lifted his head and stared into Alarick's eyes, holding his gaze.

My heart shattered, and I dropped to my knees, my body racked with shivers. "Alarick..."

Nathair hissed in annoyance. "Why aren't you dead yet?"

"What?" My head shot up, and I pulsed my magic. Nathair was right. Alarick should have been dead by now, if not from the venom in his blood, then certainly by Nathair's stare.

"Wow, you are even uglier than I imagined," Alarick muttered.

Nathair jerked back, eyes wide. "What sorcery is this?"

Alarick threw his head back and laughed. He was delirious. The venom was making him delirious. It had to be. What could he possibly find so amusing about all this?

"You!" Nathair turned his head in my direction. "*You* did this!"

I swallowed hard. What—our mating! The smile that came onto my face couldn't be helped. That's what our mating had done. It made Alarick immune to Nathair's deadly stare just as I was immune, and although he could be hurt by Nathair's venom, he could not easily be killed by it. His body would fight it just as mine did.

"Traitor! I will kill you both," Nathair hissed as he lunged for me. I shifted, thrown onto my side with Nathair wrapping around me and squeezing. I thrust my head up, smacking him under his chin. He roared and opened his mouth to sink his fangs into some part of me, but a pulse of magic thrust Nathair off me, sending him rolling into the trees. I quickly took up position beside Alarick as he stood with the scythe in his hands.

"Get ready," Alarick murmured.

Nathair's roar shook the trees before he coiled and lunged forward. He sped right for us, but I waited. Alarick sent another pulse of magic at Nathair, dropping him to the ground.

"Now, Jean!"

I sprang forward, jaws open as I sank my fangs into Nathair and pinned him to the ground. Alarick leapt through the air, bringing the scythe down in a fierce swing. Nathair's roar cut short as his head hit the ground several feet away from us, bouncing before landing with a gurgling, foul-smelling squelch. His body thrashed for several heart-beats before finally falling still.

Releasing Nathair, I shifted into my human form and tackled Alarick, the force of my body hitting his knocking him to the ground. He laughed from beneath me, his hands coming to rest on my waist.

"Hello, love."

"I thought I lost you," I cried, burying my face against his neck.

"Hush now, my darling." He petted my head soothingly, and I shut my eyes tight, taking in his warmth, his scent, the feel of him. "It's over."

"I almost killed you. After everything, I poisoned you, and—"

"Enough of that," he said sternly, moving me away so he

could look into my eyes. "Jean, you *saved* me. Your blood saved me."

I blinked at him, and he chuckled.

"That's right. Because of you, not only was I able to heal myself, but Nathair's stare didn't kill me." He booped my nose. The cad. "Also, you used my magic."

"I did?" I recalled lightning striking Nathair and a shift in the stars. "Oh Goddess above, I did, didn't I?"

He laughed, and I realized I was lying on him in the middle of a forest with a rotting basilisk head a mere few feet away. I quickly got up and helped him to his feet. "It's really over, isn't it?"

"It is now." He pointed behind me, and his children emerged from the trees. Some of them looked a little worse for wear, but they were alive. All of them. Sinopa approached us, her white attire now gray with splotches of black. Beside me, Alarick snapped his fingers and cleaned them up. She beamed brightly at him before launching herself into his arms.

"I'm happy you're not dead."

Alarick laughed. "Me too." He gazed up over her head at all his shifter children. "Thank you. Jean and I couldn't have done this without you."

Owin shrugged, a mischievous smile on his boyish face. "We know."

I laughed, surprised when Owin threw himself into my arms. For a second, I didn't know what to do. I'd never been hugged by anyone who wasn't Alarick. I tentatively wrapped my arms around him and returned his embrace, smiling at the happy sigh he let out. He squeezed me before looking up at me.

"Does this mean you're going to be the father of all shifters as well?"

I gaped at Owin, my mouth dropping open but no words coming out. Beside me, Alarick's booming laughter echoed through the forest. I held back a smile and smacked his arm. "It's a serious question, Alarick."

"Is it?" Alarick's smile sent a shiver through me, and Owin quickly stepped away, his nose wrinkled.

"Ew, the dads are getting all lovey-dovey."

Alarick arched an eyebrow at me, and I sighed. "Well, I guess that answers that question." His laughter was infectious, and I couldn't help but join in. Released by Sinopa, Alarick took my hand in his. He raised my fingers to his lips for a kiss.

"Will you rule at my side as my prince and my husband?"

I sucked in a sharp breath. "Husband?"

The cheer was deafening. Alarick put a hand up to hush everyone. "He hasn't said yes yet."

I shook my head at him. "As if there could be any other answer. Yes, Alarick. I will rule at your side as your mate, your prince, and your husband."

With a loud "whoop" Alarick threw his arms around me, lifting me off my feet. He kissed me, and the cheers around us faded as I sank into his kiss. Never in my many years on this Earth would I have imagined such happiness. My heart swelled, ready to overflow with the love I felt for this amazing, complicated, astounding creature.

"I love you," Alarick murmured against my lips.

"I love you too." I brushed my lips over his. "Let's go home."

Alarick snapped his fingers and portal after portal appeared. The shifter princes, princesses, and their mates said their goodbyes as they disappeared back to their realms, with Alarick promising to visit them soon. Each and every one would receive a gift of gratitude from us for the part they played. Once we'd seen every shifter home, Alarick took my hand in his and snapped his fingers, and the portal to our home opened before us. With the full use of my magic, I was able to see the splendor that was our palace. We stepped through and were greeted by the cheers of our staff as they rushed us.

I couldn't believe we were home. It felt as if it had been years since we'd left, but I knew it hadn't been long at all. Alarick apologized to everyone for worrying them. He was going to hold a quick meeting get them all up to date. I made to follow him to the throne room, but he turned and shook his head at me.

"You should rest. Take a warm bath in our room."

"Our room." I smiled at that. I loved Alarick's room and spent more time in there than I did my own. "Are you sure?"

"Positive." He leaned in and kissed my cheek. I wasn't sorry he was letting me skip the meeting.

As I walked down the brightly lit corridors of the palace I'd lived in for thousands of years, everything looked... new. This was the first time I'd not accompanied Alarick while he attended his duties. It was odd but somehow settling. I'd always found being at his side a pleasure. A secret delight rather than a duty, though I could have done without some of his meetings. I spent a good deal of those making certain he didn't fall asleep while his ambassadors rattled on and on as if Alarick wasn't already aware of everything that went on with his shifter children.

Entering the bedroom, I paused inside the doorway, my heart skipping a beat at the familiar sight. My eyes landed on the expansive bed, still made from the day we'd returned from Bernd's kingdom. I walked behind the couch, running my hand along the top of the backrest, remembering all the nights I'd sat here with Alarick's head on my lap. In the en suite bathroom, I turned on the faucets, running the water as I did every night. The bath was the size of a small pool, the bathroom bigger than some of the bedrooms in the palace. It was a suite built for a king, large and lavish. I tossed in a handful of Alarick's favorite aromatic bath salts before undressing.

The water was blissfully steamy, and I couldn't help my groan as I walked down the small set of steps into the bath. I waded over to the marble bench and sat with my back to the wall, letting my head rest against the ledge. The weight of the world eased off my shoulders and I sighed contentedly. For the first time in my life, true and utter peace washed over me. The threat to Alarick's life was over. My past was out in the open, and Alarick loved me. Things couldn't get any better.

"Mind if I join you?"

Or maybe they could.

I opened my eyes and let out a dreamy sigh as Alarick entered the tub.

He laughed softly. "I take it that's a yes?"

"Yes. Always yes." I sat up, moaning my delight as he brought me into his arms, and our legs tangled as he turned us so I could straddle his lap. "How was your meeting, dear?"

Alarick grinned. "I think I may have given the poor staff whiplash from how quickly I fired information at them. All I could think of was you naked in this tub."

I hummed and wrapped my arms around his neck. "Such a naughty king."

"Naughty is exactly the manner of thoughts I'm having at this very moment. But first, we wash."

I moved off him to get the sponge and his favorite shower gel. After pouring a generous amount into the sponge, I turned to wash him, only to have him gently seize my wrist.

"It's my turn to take care of you, Jean."

I started to protest, but he turned me in the water in front of him, his hand sliding around my front. On second thought, I could certainly get used to this. He pulled me back against him and nuzzled my temple as he washed me. With every swipe of the sponge, he caressed my skin with his hand. There was no part of me he didn't explore with his long, deft fingers. I laid my head back against his shoulder, a moan escaping me. His hard erection pressed into my back, and I turned to take the sponge from him.

"As much as I'm loving your attentiveness, we need to move this along, Alarick, because I need you to take me to bed."

Alarick's pupils dilated, and he ran his tongue along his bottom lip. "Right."

We made quick work of washing—there would be plenty of time to cherish each other in the bath later—then quickly dried ourselves. I'd just dropped the towel into the hamper when I was swept off my feet.

"Alarick!"

He laughed as he carried me into the bedroom and laid me on the bed. He snapped his fingers, the lights in the room turning off and the flames in the wall sconces flickering to life. The balcony doors opened on a breeze, the curtain billowing softly as the moonlight cast an ethereal glow inside the room.

"You're so very beautiful, Jean." Alarick spread my legs so he could lie between them, and my breath hitched.

"I still can't believe I'm here in your bed."

"Our bed," Alarick corrected, leaning in to kiss me. He paused before his lips reached mine. "I'm sorry, Jean. I should have asked. We don't have to move you into this room. We can choose another room, or I can have one made. You can keep your room if you wish. Am I being pushy? I'm making decisions for you again, aren't I?"

"Alarick?"

"Yes?"

"When have I ever allowed you to make a decision for me?"

He went pensive. "Um, never?"

"Correct. And in instances where you've decided something should be a certain way and I've disagreed?"

"You were right, and I conceded."

"Exactly. I don't think there's any need to worry where I'm concerned. I'm looking forward to being your husband and to having my things moved into our room. Right here."

Alarick's smile lit up his face. "I do love you so much, Jean."

"I love you too." I reached between us to take hold of his rock-hard shaft, and his eyes widened. "Now, put this beautiful cock inside me and have your way with me until I shout your name so loud everyone in this realm knows I'm yours."

A wicked gleam came into his eyes. "As you wish, my love." He kissed my cheek, then trailed kisses down my jaw, making his way down my neck as a slick finger pressed into my entrance. I gasped and arched my back up off the bed. His deep rumble of a chuckle sent a shiver through me, and I moaned as he continued to trail kisses down my body. He flicked his tongue over one nipple, and I slipped my hands into his soft hair.

"Alarick, please."

A second finger pressed inside me, and I writhed beneath him, needing more of him, to have him fill me. Nothing in this world felt better than having Alarick inside me, his weight on me, his smooth skin warm against mine. I slid a hand down over the muscles of his strong back and slowly rolled my hips, groaning as I took my pleasure, his fingers moving in and out of me as he would soon be doing.

Alarick lavished more attention on my nipples before moving his lips lower. I held on to his hair again, gasping loudly when he suddenly swallowed me whole.

"Oh Goddess, yes!"

I bucked my hips, my hard shaft surrounded by the heat of his mouth. He increased the pressure as he sucked me. I feared I would tremble apart any moment and fisted the blanket as if it were the only thing keeping me from unraveling beneath him. He continued to work his fingers inside me as he sucked, licked, and laved at my painfully hard shaft. My toes curled and my muscles tensed, lightning traveling through every inch of me.

"Alarick, I need you inside me *now*."

With a deep chuckle, he pulled off me and lined himself up. He kissed me, his tongue tangling with mine as he slowly sank inside me. My eyes all but rolled into the back of my head when he started moving. I cursed, making him laugh. It brought a smile to my face.

"You're beautiful," I whispered, cupping his face. He turned his head and kissed my palm before leaning in to kiss me again. I surrendered completely to him, giving myself up like I had never done for anyone. My mate. I still couldn't believe it. I dug my fingers into the muscles of his back as our bodies moved together.

"Jean..." Alarick's lips brushed my cheeks, my name on his lips like a whispered prayer, and my heart soared, knowing I would be cherished by him until the end of days.

For longer than I could remember, I'd stood at his side, vigilant, attentive, in love. None of that had changed, nor would it, but this time, I'd be at his side as his mate, the two of us ruling together.

Alarick snapped his hips, and I cried out, my body lighting up from the inside like a star exploding. As if sensing I was close, Alarick reached between us and pumped my leaking cock, the movement matching his hard thrusts as he pounded into me.

"Yes! Oh Goddess, yes."

"My mate. My beautiful mate." Alarick changed his angle, and a galaxy of stars exploded across my vision. I screamed out his name as my release hit me, every muscle in my body pulled tight as a storm of pleasure surged through me, a blast of colorful light bursting into the room. Alarick snapped his hips twice more before he was roaring his release, the earth seeming to tremble around us as he spilled himself inside me. The room appeared to fade away, surrounding us with twinkling stars and colorful galaxies. Peace washed over me as Alarick collapsed on me. I wrapped my arms around him and ran a hand soothingly over his hair.

I watched the stars and held him as we caught our breaths. "You better not fall asleep on me."

"I wouldn't dream of it," he replied, voice laced with sleep. He nuzzled my neck and let out a happy sigh. "You're very comfortable, though."

I smiled and closed my eyes, sleep ready to claim me as

well, when Alarick's soft-spoken words brought a light to my heart bright enough to rival the stars above.

"Thank you for choosing me, Jean. For gifting me your heart. I love you."

"And I love you." As long as the stars shone in the heavens, I would be at his side, ever vigilant, always in love.

EPILOGUE

ALARICK

That bastard was around here somewhere.

I stalked the halls, his scent still in my nostrils along with that of my delicious pastry. Or at least what had been my delicious pastry. Today this ended. I didn't survive Nathair to be bested by a bushy-tailed thief. A faint squeak met my ear, and I froze, silently lowering my huge white lion frame to the floor. My ear twitched as I listened for the faintest sound from that fiend. He couldn't be far.

Something moved from the shadows beneath the hall table, and I stalked closer, peering into the darkness. With a loud titter, the beast darted out from beneath the table, and I lunged after him, chasing him down the hall as fast as my giant fur paws could go. The little bastard was fast, I'd give him that. I sped after him, swerving around staff as they went about their duties. By now they simply whirled out of the way, not giving me a second glance. I skidded on the marble floor as I made a sharp turn, nearly slamming into the wall.

The fiend was heading for the garden. My roar shook the palace walls as I neared the open garden doors. He sped through and I followed, leaping down the stairs and landing on the grass without a sound. He darted into the maze, and I gave chase. If he thought he could outwit me, he had another think coming. Had the little thief taken up residence in my favorite tree?

In the center of the garden maze, the hedges blooming with exquisite magical flowers, grew a magnificent tree I'd planted when I first had my palace built. Its branches were never bare. At night its tiny colorful leaves twinkled and glowed like a million bright stars. In the summer I loved to nap in its shade, let the peace of the maze and the aroma of fresh flowers wash over me.

How dare this fluffy rodent invade my tree!

The culprit scurried down the trunk and stared at me before trilling noisily, chattering. I growled as I stalked closer, ready to pounce. The thief had stolen his last cinnamon bun. Lowering my body close to the grass, I stuck my lion butt in the air, tail thrashing as I prepared to make my move, but movement stilled me. Two tiny red squirrels scurried down, placing themselves on either side of the pastry thief. I blinked at them. Kits?

Flopping down onto the grass with a groan, I laid my head on my paws and grumbled. He had kits, baby squirrels. Now what? I couldn't very well vanquish the foul beast now. Not when he had two tiny foul beasts to take care of. I huffed, and all three of them scrambled to the ground, tails twitching excitedly as they launched themselves at my muzzle to pet me. What a sad state of affairs, being petted and cooed at by puffy rodents.

Fine. You win.

I grumbled, and they darted around happily. The moment I shifted, sitting on the grass, they climbed all over me.

"Yes, all right. Fine. Let's make a deal. You will be allowed to steal a total of one cinnamon bun from me out of every batch. It's bigger than you anyway. I don't even know how you manage to get it out here."

Papa squirrel tittered at me, and I waved a hand in dismissal. "I appreciate you stroking my ego, but it's not necessary. I hope you're feeding your babies more than cinnamon buns."

He squealed at me, and I put my hands up in surrender.

"Just offering some advice."

"What are you doing?"

I smiled at Jean's suspicious tone. "Nothing."

"Are you still at war with that poor squirrel?" He came to stand next to me and gaped at the three squirrels in my lap.

"We've reached... an understanding."

"I'm not sure what that means, but all right." He seemed to notice the babies and gasped. "Oh! Baby bun thieves!"

I narrowed my gaze at papa squirrel. "Hopefully they won't follow in their father's footsteps." I waved them off. "Go on now. I suspect my cinnamon bun is up in that tree somewhere. I do, however, reserve the right to chase you should I see you," I said pointedly. Papa squirrel tittered happily. "Deal."

Jean shook his head. "Never a dull moment with you, is there?"

"Are you saying you want that to change?" I brought him into my arms for a kiss, loving how he melted into me.

"Never," he murmured before his cheeks flushed. "Alarick, I have something to tell you. Or rather, show you."

He looked nervous, which was so unlike Jean. "What's the matter, love?"

"Um, something... happened."

"Are you all right? Are you hurt?" I looked him over. He seemed fine on the outside. No blood, bruises, scars.

"Yes, I mean, no, I'm fine. I'm not hurt."

"Then what is it?"

Jean dropped his gaze to his fingers before clearing his throat. "You know how we're still discovering all the changes in ourselves brought about from our mating?"

"Yes."

"Well, um... I have something to show you. Stay right here."

Jean disappeared, and I stood wondering what on earth was going on. Why was Jean acting so... strange? Several minutes went by, and I was about to go find him when he returned.

I squealed. Actually squealed. "Is that...?"

Jean beamed at me as he held up the most adorable little snake I'd ever seen. "Yes. A baby basilisk."

The baby basilisk was probably the size of a small dog. He was the sweetest, most adorable creature I'd ever seen in my life. He had big aquamarine eyes, his black irises containing the swirls of galaxies. "He has our eyes."

"And he can't kill with them. He also has no venom." Jean cradled the baby in his arms. "He's a mix of both of us." He had Jean's black scales, and they shimmered in the sunlight, along with a small crown on his head. Instead of green fur on his mane and tail, it was the same snow white as my mane in my lion form. The baby shifted into human form, and I melted into a puddle, or at least felt as if I had. He had chubby cheeks, dark hair, and big bright eyes. I didn't know what was more beautiful, the baby or the look on Jean's face as he held him.

"How?" I asked, stroking the baby's velvety soft cheek.

"I don't know. Remember this morning how I felt tired and took a nap?"

I nodded. I'd been concerned Jean was coming down with something.

"I remember thinking as I fell asleep, how sad it was to be the last of my kind. How lovely it would be if there could be basilisks that weren't evil killers, but good. When I woke up, there he was, lying next to me. He just sort of... appeared."

"You made him, Jean."

Jean stared at me. "What do you mean, I made him?" He patted his belly. "That's not something I can do, Alarick." His eyes went huge. "Or is it?"

I laughed softly at his scandalized expression. "No, darling. Not like that. How do you think all my shifter children came to be? I didn't actually birth them. I dreamed them and thought about them, designed them ever so carefully with all the love in my heart for them, taking into account every detail in their creation. And then they were born." I cooed at the sweet boy, my heart ready to burst when he gurgled and giggled.

"A new basilisk prince," Jean said quietly, lifting the baby to kiss his head.

"What should we name him?"

"What about Asier? It means *the beginning*."

"I love that. And I love you, Asier." I kissed the top of his head, then kissed Jean. "And you."

Asier shifted into his basilisk form, and Jean laughed softly. "I think he's trying to control his shift. Don't worry, little one. You will, in time." Jean placed Asier on the grass, and he slithered and bounced happily. Thankfully we had plenty of room in the center of the maze as Jean shifted, his basilisk form taking up all the space around us. Asier was the size of the green tuft on Jean's tail, making me laugh. Jean lowered his head to the grass, and I shifted into my huge white lion form. Nuzzling Jean's head, I flopped down onto the grass beside him.

Asier bumped his little nose against Jean's before slithering happily away, then speeding back and bumping Jean's nose again. Were I in my human form, I would be laughing. Asier was too adorable. Once he'd worn himself out, he slithered over to me and stretched his little body up. I lowered my head, and he nuzzled my face before crawling up my body and burying himself under tufts of my mane. He poked his little head out and closed his eyes.

With a happy groan, Jean coiled his large body around me, eyes drifting shut. In all my years alive, I never imagined I would find the perfect mate, much less end up with a family. My heart swelled with love, and I knew I would do anything to protect them. Jean and Asier were basilisk princes, the only two in existence. I would see to it they were always protected, happy, and aware of how much I adored them every second of every day.

My boys. My loves. My heart.

A NOTE FROM THE AUTHOR

THANK you so much for reading *The King and His Vigilant Valet*, the third book in the Paranormal Princes series. I hope you enjoyed King Alarick and Jean's adventures, and if you did, please consider leaving a review on Amazon. Reviews can have a significant impact on a book's visibility, so any support you show these fellas would be amazing.

Want to stay up-to-date on my releases and receive exclusive content? Sign up for my newsletter.

Follow me on Amazon to be notified of a new release, or connect with me on social media, including my Facebook group, Donuts, Dog Tags, and Day Dreams, where we chat books, post pictures, have giveaways, and more!

Looking for inspirational photos of my books? Visit my book boards on Pinterest.

Thank you again for joining the fellas on their adventures. We hope to see you real soon!

ALSO BY CHARLIE COCHET

FOUR KINGS SECURITY

Love in Spades

Be Still My Heart

Join the Club

Diamond in the Rough

FOUR KINGS SECURITY UNIVERSE

Beware of Geeks Bearing Gifts

LOCKE AND KEYES AGENCY

Kept in the Dark

PARANORMAL PRINCES

The Prince and His Bedeviled Bodyguard

The Prince and His Captivating Carpenter

The King and His Vigilant Valet

THIRDS

Hell & High Water

Blood & Thunder

Rack & Ruin

Rise & Fall

Against the Grain

Catch a Tiger by the Tail

Smoke & Mirrors

Thick & Thin

Darkest Hour Before Dawn

Gummy Bears & Grenades

Tried & True

THIRDS BEYOND THE BOOKS

THIRDS Beyond the Books Volume 1

THIRDS Beyond the Books Volume 2

THIRDS UNIVERSE

Love and Payne

COMPROMISED

Center of Gravity

NORTH POLE CITY TALES

Mending Noel

The Heart of Frost

The Valor of Vixen

Loving Blitz

Disarming Donner

Courage and the King

North Pole City Tales Complete Series Paperback

SOLDATI HEARTS

The Soldati Prince

The Foxling Soldati

LITTLE BITE OF LOVE

An Intrepid Trip to Love

Healing Hunter's Heart

STANDALONE

Forgive and Forget

AUDIOBOOKS

Check out the audio versions on Audible here.

ABOUT THE AUTHOR

Charlie Cochet is the international bestselling author of the THIRDS series. Born in Cuba and raised in the US, Charlie enjoys the best of both worlds, from her daily Cuban latte to her passion for classic rock.

Currently residing in Central Florida, Charlie is at the beck and call of a rascally Doxiepoo bent on world domination. When she isn't writing, she can usually be found devouring a book, releasing her creativity through art, or binge watching a new TV series. She runs on coffee, thrives on music, and loves to hear from readers.

www.charliecochet.com

Sign up for Charlie's newsletter:
https://newsletter.charliecochet.com

facebook.com/charliecochet

twitter.com/charliecochet

instagram.com/charliecochet

pinterest.com/charliecochet

bookbub.com/authors/charliecoche

goodreads.com/CharlieCochet